W9-BLV-289

60

FARRAR
STRAUS
GIROUX

GET
DOWN

GET DOWN

STORIES

asali solomon

farrar, straus and giroux
new york

Farrar, Straus and Giroux
19 Union Square West, New York 10003

Copyright © 2006 by Asali Solomon
All rights reserved
Distributed in Canada by Douglas & McIntyre Ltd.
Printed in the United States of America
First edition, 2006

Library of Congress Cataloging-in-Publication Data
Solomon, Asali.
    Get down : stories / Asali Solomon. —1st ed.
        p.   cm.
    ISBN-13: 978-0-374-29942-2 (hardcover : alk. paper)
    ISBN-10: 0-374-29942-0 (hardcover)
    1. African American young men—Fiction.   I. Title.

PS3619.04335G47 2006
813′.6—dc22
                                                    2006024677

Designed by Michelle McMillian

www.fsgbooks.com

1   3   5   7   9   10   8   6   4   2

For James, Rochelle,
and Akiba Solomon, with love

THIS CAN'T BE LIFE.

—Jay-Z

contents

twelve takes thea

my mother and father, the only kids to go to college in their large families, believed deeply that they could only have genius children. When my older brother, Stephen, was assigned to the fourth-grade slow learners' class at Franklin Elementary for his habit of staring at the floor, it set into motion a chain of events that would end, for me, with a partial scholarship to the Barrett School for Girls. Every day I got up at 6:00 a.m. and rode a school bus from Southwest Philadelphia to a sprawling campus in Bryn Mawr, Pennsylvania. Stephen got a tutor and transferred to a better public elementary. I got a school with its own coat of arms.

My first friend at Barrett when I started there in second grade was a girl called Jane, who had light brown hair, so Stephen began calling me Jane. Even after the girl had left the school and moved away, Stephen continued to remind me how much of a Jane I was becoming when I was excited or angry or got in the way of his frequent mood swings. This continued even after the fourth grade, when another black girl came to my class and we became best friends.

Hearing our two names together—The-a Brown, Nad-ja

Bell—was how I learned about poetic meter and internal rhyme. One day our English teacher, Mr. Edwards, put aside Emily Dickinson and chanted our two names several times. He clapped staccato beats and looked proud of himself. Nadja wore a blank expression, and I tried not to smile.

As we walked away from the classroom, Nadja said, "You know he can't tell us apart, right?" and that was true and sad, so it made me laugh. A bland girl named Stephanie Simon, who was walking alone, looked at us with curiosity. When I saw her looking, I laughed even harder.

You could barely breathe in the space between me and Nadja. I might have been a shrill thing, but my best friend was cool, like a villain on a detective show. Once, in the locker room after swimming, Allison Evans announced, "I heard there's pools of blood on every corner in Philadelphia."

I clutched a towel to me and couldn't think of anything to say except "Well, well."

Nadja, already dry and dressed, closed her locker with a definitive click. "I guess that's why there's taxes for street cleaning."

Before Nadja, I had a few friends who were loyal to me at lunchtime, though we had nothing to talk about. I waved discreetly to the black girls scattered in other grades, and smiled at the hairnetted black lunch ladies who ladled me extra soup. I threw a party, and nobody from school came. With Nadja, I had someone to sit and eat with, and somebody in the world besides my grandpa Theo called my house to speak to me.

Sometimes on Fridays after school I went over to Nadja's, where we'd listen to the Power Four at Four on Power 99, and she'd teach me the new dances she'd learned from the older girls who lived on her block. Each of those afternoons, just before six o'clock, we'd turn off the music, dab away our sweat, and spread our books out on the dining-room table. Nadja's mother believed that dancing was for adults and that secular music was from Satan. Those were the days of Rick James and of Prince's "Erotic City," so I guess she was right.

AT THE END of sixth grade, I learned that Nadja's mother was transferring her to Saint Mary's in South Philly. Her mother had recently married a minister who thought his stepdaughter should go to a Christian school.

Nadja told me the news on a chilly spring day. We wore sweatpants under our gray uniform kilts and twisted up the swings after lunch. "It's not like there's anything I can do," she said.

"Well, did you even try?"

"I just told you I did. My mom kept saying, 'The more you complain about going down there, the more me and Mr. Al know you need to do it.'"

"But Barrett was okay all these years."

Nadja stared ahead. "Yeah, well, now he's gotta pay part of it. And I overheard them talking the other night—it's a lot cheaper."

I wrinkled my nose, hating Mr. Al, whom I'd never met.

"Oh, does your mom know how *sadistic* the nuns are?" I asked. I had learned this word from my mom's best friend, a Catholic school graduate.

Nadja looked at me blankly.

I embellished on what I'd heard about girls getting whipped and humiliated by the Sisters, and I added some Barrett snobbery. "You know it's going to be a bunch of mallchicks and skanks, and you're gonna start using a lot of hair spray and going to dances with Guidos—"

Nadja halted the lazy motion of her swing. "Thea, this is not helping me. Anyway, I already use a little bit of hair spray." She pushed at the sides of her pulled-back hair.

I also made my swing stop. "Well, maybe I could get my mom to transfer me too."

She smirked. "Your parents would never let you go anywhere white people get to beat you."

That afternoon on the school bus, I planned to go home and look injured until my parents asked me what was wrong. Instead I ran to meet my mother at the door and told her Nadja was leaving me.

Mom paused at the door, listening. Then, as if snapping out of a trance, she hung her jacket, slammed the closet door, and sorted a stack of mail into two piles.

"Thea, I'm sorry," she said, and kissed me on the top of my head. "I'm sure you all will stay friends. I have got to get out of this skirt!" Her voice was cheerful, but her back was to me, as she was already on the stairs. I went to the living room and flopped onto her huge velvet chair.

"What am I going to do without Nadja?" I asked as soon as she came down in one of her many sweat suits.

"Thea, you'll be fine," she said, shooing me out of her chair with a weak smile. "Maybe Barrett will get some new black students. Tell you the truth, though," she said, as if I couldn't hear her, "I really don't know what Reba is thinking, sending her down there with that white trash."

"What?"

"You'll be fine."

Later, I followed my father into the kitchen, where he made omelets for dinner. I leaned onto his whisking arm and addressed his neatly rolled shirtsleeve. "What am I going to do at Barrett without Nadja?"

"Well," he said, and gently pushed me back up to standing. "You're not there to socialize. You'll do what you've been doing—bringing home A's. *Yeah.*"

At dinner, Stephen gave his opinion.

"Now you're really gonna be a wannabe *Jane.*" Incidentally, Nadja was the sole Barrett girl my brother didn't call Jane.

Stephen made me so mad that my head was a blender full of blood. Sometimes, when my parents weren't around, I pulled off the do-rag he wore at home or called him a faggot. He hated that.

"Let your sister be, Stephen," my mother said in a firm voice, though sometimes when he called me Jane she looked amused.

Neither of my parents answered me. They couldn't tell me who I would walk everywhere with, or what would I do when I was finished lunch and everyone separated into twos and the occasional three. Worst of all, Barrett dances started in seventh grade. When Nadja told me she was leaving, I couldn't help picturing myself at one. Again and again I saw myself stuck to the wall of the main auditorium. All the girls in our class and a bunch of boys from Braeford Prep were in the center of the room under a disco ball, a writhing throng of pale arms and legs tangled up in each other, closing ranks.

I SPENT THAT SUMMER in a sulky cloud. Between sessions of painting and computer camp, where I refused to talk to any of the kids beyond "hi" or "bye," I curled up in my mom's chair and read Lois Duncan books. My favorite was about twins. One of the twins was evil and developed the ability to leave her body using something called astral projection. Her evil had landed her in a mental institution. While there, she worked on using her power to locate the happy normal twin, trying to get possession of her body. The book, from which I was hoping to learn astral projection, was the best way to get my mind off of being alone at Barrett.

I read some happier non–Lois Duncan books too, like the Tracie Marie series. In both of the ones I read, *Tracie Marie Turns Ten* and *Tracie Marie Takes Twelve*, the same thing happened. Girls who thought they were unpopular discovered that actually, the cute guy liked them and the most interesting other girls wanted to be their friends. Whenever I caught myself fantasizing about a sudden change along these lines, I was annoyed enough to punch my own arm.

The first day of seventh grade was hot and gold with sunshine. I tried to gaze moodily out of my bedroom window like one of the young heroines in my books, but I saw only the frosted bathroom window of the house across the alley. I dressed slowly until my mother yelled down the hall that it was time to rock and roll.

I hated it when she said that.

As if to fill the hole in our lives left by Nadja, there were four new girls in seventh grade. This was more than we'd ever got in a year, and it brought our number to thirty. I thought of the new girls as flavors of ice cream or contestants in the Miss Universe pageant. Lisa DeKulis had red hair and one crazy eyebrow, and Belle Everett had a loose blond 'fro that reminded me of Jessica

Lange in *King Kong.* There was also Frances Dyson and Beth Johanssen.

Frances was black. I knew that my parents would be very excited about this. But when I laid eyes on her, my heart dove right into my feet. It wasn't the first time I was nagged by the thought that maybe Stephen was right and I did have the sensibilities of a Jane.

Frances's hair was in stacks, an intricate tilt-a-whirl, like the hair of the girls I saw in my neighborhood. Like Nadja, I usually pulled mine back. Because my mom, who wore ornate cornrows, didn't let me get a perm or use hair products with alcohol, mine was a little unwieldy. But the point was, we didn't look so *ghetto.*

Frances certainly didn't mind looking ghetto. To prove it, she wore heavy gold door-knocker hoops with the name *Frances* running the span in between.

She wore the blue kilt, which no one wore because of its unflattering length. I felt bad that no one had told her. But she was entirely to blame, I thought, for wearing Reeboks instead of Tretorns.

When I saw Frances, I thought of something that happened in my first year at Barrett. Allison "blood pools" Evans stood next to me in the bathroom mirror. She said, "Do this," and puckered her lips. I imitated her. She laughed and clapped, and I noticed that her lips were a pale pink line, while mine swelled outside of some invisible margin. Frances, and not because of her lips, reminded me of that moment.

Though I knew she'd seek me out, I almost jumped when she fell into step with me on my way to the dining room. I was walking with Stephanie Simon, who, like me, had lost her best friend to another school. Stephanie was talking about her summer near Rhode Island and the tastiness of something called cod balls. It sounded unlikely.

"How do you find anything here?" Frances was suddenly between us. The halls in the old building were narrow, so Stephanie dropped back. I walked with Frances, thinking that she sounded as if one of us had specifically done her wrong.

"Uhmm," I said.

I didn't want to be overly friendly to Frances, especially in front of other people. I didn't want them to assume that we were going to be best friends and then leave us alone like me and Nadja. I mean, sometimes the two of us had acquired a third, like a barnacle, but it was always somebody who wanted to take my best friend, and I made it clear that this was never going to happen. Anyway, it had been easier and safer for us to stick together. Then we didn't have to ache alone over their slick, cushy homes with rooms in the tens. Together, Nadja and I faced the shame of meeting their black housekeepers, who had no last names. But I knew there'd be only double the weakness in the teaming of me and Frances.

Stephanie said, "Well, the halls really only go toward the dining room or back toward the middle school."

Frances looked back at her, then darted her eyes suspiciously at the low ceilings and stained-glass windows.

"You know, it took me a while to find my way too," I said.

I made my voice bright. I was not going to be mean. The question was how much I had to *befriend* Frances. I was caught between the other girls—who, I felt, would not understand her at all—and my parents, who would want us handcuffed together. Eventually, the Black Barrett Parents (the BBPs) were going to get together, and if my parents went to the first meeting, or tea as it was sometimes called, and met Frances's parents, and if there was any indication that I wasn't carrying her on my back, saving her seats, or showing her how to flush the antique middle school toilets, I would be very sorry.

Of course my parents wouldn't be that interested in any new Indian girls in my grade that year. If they had, I would have had the pleasure of telling them about Beth Johanssen. Instead, I told them briefly about Frances at dinner, and I called Nadja directly afterward.

"Isn't that crazy?" I asked her. "Beth Johanssen."

"She must be adopted," Nadja said dreamily. She had always been fascinated by adoption. She couldn't see why people tried so hard to have their own children when they could create more interesting families with other people's kids.

"I don't know about that," I said. "Maybe her parents changed her name from . . ."—I couldn't think of an Indian name—"because they're sellouts."

"You sound like Stephen," Nadja said. "I bet she's adopted. She probably thinks she's white."

I felt sure that Beth both knew and felt lucky that she was not white. She was taller than most of us, about Nadja's height I thought, and slim, with a respectable chest. She wore her straight black hair in a neat ponytail, and when she couldn't hear you, she wrinkled her perfect, skinny nose. "Sorry?" she said, which I started to do. Her eyes were a lighter brown than her reddish skin, an electrifying contrast. Even wearing some off-brand of tennis shoe, she was clearly the prettiest girl in the class. I did not mention this part to Nadja.

"Don't go get a new best friend" was what I said.

Though I allowed Frances to shadow me for the first couple of weeks of school, I made sure to sit next to or near to Beth Johanssen in both English and algebra. Before I casually made my way over to her, I'd watch her put down her red knapsack, retie her tunic, readjust her ponytail, and sit. I never knew why she didn't fix herself up in the girl's room, but I decided she was the type of girl who would answer every why with a why not.

Frantic to get her to really talk to me, I looked all around and at her things. A collage of models in generally unwearable clothes covered her notebook. I asked her where she got the pictures.

"*Vogue*," she said. "September is the best issue."

"How long did it take you to make that collage—uh—thing?" I asked, even boring myself.

Beth shrugged. "Couple hours."

Finally Mrs. Langley walked in, wearing, to my joy, sheer stockings.

"Beth," I whispered. It was the first time I said her name. "Look at her legs."

Mrs. Langley had a remarkable amount of body hair. Her stockings were a picture of arrested motion, not unlike tall, windswept grass.

Beth's eyes widened. "Oh my God," she said out of the side of her mouth. This was how we became friends.

I later understood that anyone in the class could tell a similar story of becoming friends with Beth. She had private jokes with just about all of us, even the three most popular girls in the class, Liza, Lizzie, and Rachel. This was especially impressive to me because I felt leaden and mute around those girls. I couldn't remember where I had learned this reverence. It felt ancient. In the

Tracie Marie series, the popular kids at Tracie's school were the kindest, most attractive, and smartest students. At Barrett it was an indefinable something else. Lizzie was stocky and bucktoothed, with scraggly strawberry blond hair and a semipermanent frown. Liza had smooth skin and clear brown eyes, but she was afflicted with a nervous laugh that always ended in a snort. Still, these were the girls everyone wanted to be.

Beth didn't follow them around. She seemed content enough to sit or whisper with them occasionally at lunch or in study hall. Other times, she whispered with any old Jane, me for example. Because our first real conversation was about Mrs. Langley, Beth's private joke with me was that everyone at Barrett looked like an animal.

Mrs. Langley was obviously an ape, she said, "but maybe hairier."

Stephanie Simon was a moose because she had an upturned nose and large teeth.

"Horse?" I offered, because you could get into trouble at Barrett if you weren't careful who you talked about, or to.

She smirked. "No way. Horses are beautiful. I have one on my grandmother's farm," she said, biting a chewed-up thumbnail. "Definitely moose."

In the precious few minutes before algebra and French, we thought of new ones. Jennifer Morris—pit bull. Jo Lydell—turtle. Becky Alberts, poor Becky, with dark tangled hair, thick chunks of something called *psoriasis*, and a voice filled with spit (that was always talking about Doctor Who)—

"Monster," Beth decided. "Is that an animal?"

I was always relieved when I saw Beth and she remembered

that we had a thing. On the day that Frances was moved into our algebra class, Beth's eyes sparkled. She scrawled on a piece of paper and pushed it onto my desk. "Monkey."

TALKING TO FRANCES was like pushing a heavy grocery cart with a trick wheel. We spoke about things like what our mothers did (mine ran a Head Start program at the Malcolm X Housing Projects, and hers was an executive secretary) and what we watched on television (she loved *Good Times*, which I wasn't allowed to watch). She was from a neighborhood in North Philly near my mom's job, a place that made my mother shake her head. Frances and I didn't intersect at any point, and we didn't make each other laugh.

Another difference between us was that Frances was extraordinarily smart. I worked hard and made A's, but Frances always seemed to know exactly what our teachers were trying to get us to understand. This caused me trouble with Beth. Each time Frances spoke up in class, Beth rolled her eyes at me. I silently begged Frances to slow down her campaign of academic domination, but there she was, publicly racking up extra credit, winning our weekly journal contest, reading aloud an A-plus paper on the war between conscience and passion in *Jane Eyre*. Frances, her hair now in an even more asymmetrical Tilt-A-Whirl, wildly waving her hand, offering to help Beth out of a jam with negative numbers. Beautiful Beth at the board, with an expression so nonchalant it had to be forced, one hand on her hip, the other raised with chalk to take Frances's dictation.

Mrs. Langley practically swooned. "Great work, Frances!" Teachers were really happy about Frances being so smart. "You too, Beth," she added after a long beat.

Beth sat. She slipped me a note when Mrs. Langley turned her back to us:

Monkeys > humans at math.

I wanted to say that Frances was not a monkey, that Beth was breaking the rules of the game, which was based on the fact that people looked like all kinds of animals, not the ones you would expect. Couldn't Frances look like a lemur or a yak? I wanted to say that, but I didn't.

Beth Johanssen and I didn't just say mean things about people. She talked about how Barrett girls were nicer than her old classmates at the coed Quaker school down the road. "A lot of people hated me there," she told me once at lunch. When I asked her why, she just gave a sad little shrug. I told her about Nadja then, so we could be sad together.

"She sounds cool," she said. "We should all hang out sometime."

I agreed. But since Saint Mary's had started, it seemed like I called Nadja at all the wrong times: she was doing her homework, out at pep squad, or on her way to meet up with her new friends. We did go to the last and worst of the John Hughes movies, and I felt responsible for suggesting it, but mostly Nadja was at Saint Mary's or with Saint Mary's girls. When I asked if I could come along, she said things like "There's not space in Kelly's mom's car" or "Do you even have a fake ID?" Anyway, the descriptions of her new friends made me nervous. They had boyfriends and smoked Newports—in seventh grade. Just their names—Kelly, Sheila, and Tiffany—made me sure they wouldn't like me very much.

"We never hang out anymore," I said to her one night. I finally got her after leaving two messages on her new private answering machine. I had to use the phone in the living room, so I kept my voice low. I could tell from the taut look of the newspaper in my mom's hands that she was listening.

"Don't be like that," Nadja said. "It's just hard being at different schools." I could barely understand her. It sounded like she was eating firecrackers.

"But I've barely seen you since the summer," I said. "You never want to go anywhere with me." I did not like, but could not stop, the wheedling in my voice.

"Oh, knock it off," she snapped. "Don't make me feel bad, Thea. I didn't even want to go to this school. It's ugly and it smells and our classes are *so* boring. Then, the white girls look cheap, but they treat us like *we're* trash."

"Oh my God! What do they do to you?"

Nadja paused. "Well, I mean, it doesn't matter," she said. Then she stopped crunching and spoke more quickly. "But look, you and me, we don't have to see each other every day to be friends."

"You mean best friends?"

My mother folded the paper.

" 'Course."

Then Nadja told me the strange tale of the school's one black nun. I felt good noticing that we hung up a full hour and a half after we started talking.

"You miss Nadja, huh?" my mom said.

"I guess."

"Well, what about Frances?" The hope in my mother's eyes was about proportional to the despair I felt about Frances.

IN THE MEANTIME, my parents were off to the fall BBP meeting, one of the usual two for the year. My parents always tried to schedule more, I suspect, because they wanted another opportunity to feel politically superior to the other black parents. Many of the BBPs were the type who lived in ratty Philadelphia suburbs in an effort to say that they did not live in the city. After the very first meeting my dad had said, "They can go broke buying a little piece of house just to be smelling white people's shit— excuse me, baby—if they want. We're going to own this place before you finish college." He had gestured to a cream-colored kitchen wall dotted with grease stains that we had probably inherited from previous owners.

My parents met Frances's mom at a Saturday afternoon BBP tea. I had heard about it all week because my parents grumbled about driving all the way up to *that* Debra Brown's house in *East Hell*. Debra was the mother of Janice Brown, who was two years below me. Debra was originally from Alabama, but she spoke in clipped syllables. Janice had once told me that according to her mom, the city of Philadelphia was no place to have a family.

"I have one," I'd said, and she looked confused.

Frances's mother came alone. Apparently the father lived in North Carolina with his first and only wife and their children. Ms. Dyson had one relative in the city, a brother who was under no circumstances allowed to be in the same room with her daughter.

"Why?" I asked, and my parents looked at each other.

"She's from North Carolina," my mother repeated. "Her name is a combination of her parents' names: Roberta and Alvin."

"Ralvin?" I said.

My mother just looked at me.

"Alverta," my father said, as if he actually liked the sound of it.

I wanted them to rhapsodize over Beth's parents, though they were still unseen and racially unaccounted for. I myself wanted to ask Beth about the Johanssens, but I got the feeling she did not want to explain why she was apparently Indian and named as she was. I tried to get close by telling her that my parents belonged to an organization for the black parents of Barrett, and asking if her mom and dad knew the other Indian parents. She started to say something and then just said no.

Meanwhile, there was a new development regarding Frances that I had to report at home. About a month into school, she started speaking in a high voice that sounded hard to maintain. She had also adopted a habit of using people's names in a pointed way, as in "Are you walking to lunch, *Beckeeee?*" or "*Jooooo*, how are you feeling?"

"She's so weird," I told my parents one night. We sat in the living room, where they checked over Stephen's and my homework after dinner. I perched on the arm of my mom's chair while my brother and father slouched on the wide sofa.

"Like, totally weird," echoed Stephen, sounding not unlike the new Frances.

"What do you mean, she's weird?" my mother asked. "People say your dad's weird because he likes to cook."

"No, Sharon. People say I'm weird because I *hate* to cook, but I always wind up in your kitchen."

"No, listen," I said. "She started talking in this crazy voice, really high and proper."

"I guess she's trying to adjust," my mother said. "I wonder if her mother knows about this."

"Alverta's got enough on her mind," answered my father. They held each other's eyes.

"What?" I asked. "What are you talking about?"

I got no information and I had no rights. Since the friendship wasn't moving fast enough for them, my parents arranged with Ms. Dyson that Frances and I would spend a Friday afternoon at her house, and then I'd have dinner over there. I later learned that this visit was conceived as a pilot program leading to a regular series.

The Dyson house was walled in dark wood and mirrors. I tried not to stare at a velvet picture of an Afro'ed woman with large breasts or at the many framed portraits of Frances and her mom. As I sat down on their leather couch, Frances immediately picked up a large white-and-gold old-fashioned-style phone.

"Why don't you play some Atari," she said, pointing at a joystick. "I can't talk to my boyfriend when my mom is home."

"You have a boyfriend?"

"Is Kelvin there?" she asked sweetly.

I didn't have Atari at my house, but had learned some basics at slumber parties. Good thing too, because Frances took the phone into the kitchen and unpropped the swinging door so that it would shut. Though I couldn't really hear her conversation, a boisterous laugh I'd never heard before escaped a few times. I realized I hadn't heard her laugh much at Barrett.

I tried to turn down the beeps and squeaks on my game without being too obvious. I heard phrases: "Just you . . . Stop . . . No, stop! . . . She don't know . . . You better not." My little man fell off the steps he was jumping, because I was listening so intently. I had achieved some record low scores when Frances hung up and swung back into the living room with a bag of Oreos and two cans of soda.

"You going to the dance?" I asked as if I surely did not care, keeping my eye on game seven. I had become passionately curious about Frances in the last fifteen minutes.

She twisted her face. "Please," she said, waving her hand. "Kelvin wouldn't let me. If my mom lets us, I'm going to his homecoming."

"He's in high school?" I almost screamed.

"So what?" she said. She leaned over to the stereo cabinet and turned on the Power Four. "You really like those white girls enough to be all dancing around with them?"

I shrugged. "Don't you like anybody there?"

"Not really. I have a lot of girlfriends up on Twenty-third that go to my church." Without turning off the stereo, Frances picked up the remote, turned on the television, and stared straight ahead at it.

I had an urge to talk to her about Nadja. Instead I asked, "Why did you start talking like that?" She was speaking normally now, though just two hours ago she was hurting my throat with her falsetto.

She slowly turned her head toward me. "Like what?"

I knew I shouldn't keep talking, but I did. "You know, that voice you do at school."

An invisible shade lowered over her face. "Like, oh my God, why do you talk like this?" she shrieked.

I wanted to say something about her stupid ghetto hair and her cheap jewelry, but she had a real social life and a boyfriend. Besides, I was in her house.

"I don't talk like that, Frances."

"I don't talk like that, Frances!" she mimicked. "This is you," she said, picking up an Oreo.

My bottom lip trembled, so I bit it. Just then Ms. Dyson opened the door and stalked in on heels that were Tina Turner–high.

"Hey, you all! How's it going? Girl, let me get one of those cookies." Standing above Frances, she took the cookie out of her hand and popped it into her mouth. She kissed her daughter's palm and winked at me.

"WELL," SAID MY MOTHER that night when I told her that Frances had called me an Oreo. Then she just said it again. "Well." She woke me the next morning for an unscheduled shopping trip in honor of the dance.

When we came back from the department store, she made me model my outfit for my father and Stephen. I had gotten black patent leather loafers, a new purple sweater, matching stockings, and a black denim skirt. I descended into the living room to my parents' oohs and ahs and Stephen's silence. I executed a spin and a deliberately bad moonwalk.

"Are there going to be any black boys there?" Mom asked, her head resting on my father's shoulder. I shrugged hard, the way Beth would have, and said I didn't know.

I went upstairs to change back into my Saturday chores T-shirt. When I came down, I heard my mother speaking quietly.

"—could take your sister."

"What?" I heard Stephen say. His response to anything he didn't want to hear was "What?"

"Boy, you heard me. You could take your sister to some of your dances."

I froze out of sight on the stairs.

"But she's only in the seventh grade! She can't go to a high school dance," my brother said, whining but reasonable.

"Yeah, Mom," I said, coming down to them. "What are you trying to turn me into?" I debated whether or not to tell them about Frances's high school boyfriend and make it good, when Stephen continued.

"Anyway," he said, glaring at me, "she can't wait to have some corny white boy feelin' all up—"

"Shut up, you faggot pussy!" I yelled, saying the worst I could, but immediately calculating that this was a mistake. First of all, Stephen's face had turned from pissed to sober and sorry. Second, my mother had the pop-eyed look she got only a couple of times a year. Third, my father had moved from a seated and cuddling position to a vertical stance where he could hold my arm with his vise grip of a hand.

"Have you lost your goddamned mind?" he was saying. "What is wrong with you? You can't say something because your little rich friends say it!" He gave my arm a shake and dropped it. Then he paced in a small circle, shaking his head.

I sat down next to my mom and started hiccuping. "I'm sorry," I said in a sob.

She pulled me close. "Oh, honey, honey, it'll be okay. What is it? You miss Nadja?"

Stephen was right, but he was wrong. To have one of the Braeford boys standing over me, asking me to dance, was only the first part of the dream. It would be a faceless blue-eyed blond, a nameless brown-eyed brunet. It had to be a white boy, not one of the token black ones, that would get me to the part of the fantasy I lingered in before I went to sleep. That was when I took the boy's hand and glanced to my right, where Beth was sitting. We would lock eyes, and I would understand that she was filled with jealousy. She was jealous of me for being chosen and jealous of him for being close to me. I lay in bed one night and actually did, I punched myself in the other arm.

WE AGREED to meet there at 7:20, but Beth was going to ride with other people who lived in Paoli. I rode from the city alone with my mom.

The dance was in the volleyball gym, a big room on the edge of Middle Field, with smooth white walls and floors. As I'd seen it only in the daylight, the dim lighting was eerie and made the room look like an ice rink. Someone, probably the silver-haired and limping black maintenance man, had put away the net and lined the walls with chairs.

The first person I saw when I entered was Becky Alberts's mother, who looked like a Van Halen video girl in a tight red sweaterdress. She had lots of wavy blond hair that was brown last

time I saw her. Evidently on chaperone duty, she spoke animat-
edly to her daughter, and I didn't know whether to feel sorrier for
her or for Becky for getting stuck with each other.

In the corner, a DJ from Wheels of Steel wore the thin white
tie and pushed-up jacket sleeves of a jerk. At 7:21, Stephanie
Simon and Lisa DeKulis were already dancing to "Freeze
Frame." Chatting boys clumped in a corner where we usually
lined up to serve the ball. One of them was black and looked
pleasing from a distance. He had a shag haircut and was only a
little shorter than me. Though the other boys wore sneakers and
T-shirts, he wore a suit jacket. As I moved past for the first of nu-
merous trips to the bathroom, I glanced over at him. He did not
meet my gaze.

Without being ecstatic, I approved of myself in the mirror.
Part of my hair was in a ponytail, and the back part was out over
my shoulders. My mother had carefully blow-dried it and
daubed me with a bit of lipstick. Her perfume, a tiny bottle that
she received every other year for her wedding anniversary, was
off-limits, but she let me use the lotion that went with it. I cheerfully sniffed my wrist while I loitered over the sink and checked
my watch. I marched myself out of the bathroom at 7:35 and almost slammed into Becky Alberts, who was dripping tears onto
her oversize Doctor Who T-shirt.

I saw Liza and Lizzie—minus Rachel, who'd been going her
own way lately. I sucked in my next breath hard when I saw that
they were standing at the wall with Beth. She hadn't mentioned
that she'd be riding with *them*. And not only did she look gor-
geous, her hair fanned out over her shoulders, she also looked
happy. And not fake Barrett that's-so-awesome happy, but birthday and Saturday-morning happy. I guessed that she, Liza, and

Lizzie had gotten ready together, when all I'd had was my mother—and also Stephen, who would only say, "You don't look ugly, so stay away from nasty white boys." I kept my back straight and got ready to smile. I ventured up to her.

"Oh, hey, you made it. You look nice," she said, looking me up and down. Then she went back to her conversation.

Two boys came up on either side of Liza and Lizzie. One looked like a tall blond mop, with a Braeford blazer over a T-shirt. The other had huge glasses and skinny arms. I started to walk away, but Beth called, "Where are you going?"

I stopped in my tracks like a character in a movie and almost skipped back to her.

We danced in large, ragged circles of girls to "Don't You Want Me," "Shout," and "The Reflex." I missed Nadja and practicing the snake. We were not good dancers, but we were better than the average Barrett girl.

Beth, on the other hand, was like the other Janes, moving between the beats with flailing arms. I tried to do what she did. It was okay. It was my life, and I let myself get sweaty.

"Now we're going to slow it down a little," announced the DJ as Atlantic Starr swelled out of the speakers, "and happy birthday, Allison!" We hooted for Allison's birthday. Beth announced that she was sitting down, and I followed her toward the wall.

Before this moment, there had been the odd couple here and there. Now nearly all of the guys were on the floor with partners. The one black kid danced first with Nancy Chin, then with Jennifer Morris, whose extremely thick dark hair made her look ethnic to him, I guessed. Neither of those girls was pretty. I knew what he was doing.

I wasn't surprised that no one asked me to dance, but I

couldn't understand why Beth was sitting. Even Becky Alberts's mother danced with our biology teacher.

As the next song sobbed on, Beth said, "Thea, I have to tell you something."

My heart thrilled in the pause.

"Liza's dad beats her mom."

Whoa.

"It's true," she said, biting her thumb.

"How do you know? She told you that?"

"Sort of. She said that they fought a lot, and then tonight I got a ride with her, and her mom had a black eye, and also her dad kept yelling."

"What did he say?"

"I don't remember exactly, but it was stuff like, 'Don't you know anything, you dummy?' "

I tried to imagine that scene. It was true that Liza's mom was small, with tightly drawn skin and a frozen smile, and that her father was heavy, with little eyes and thick eyebrows. I couldn't picture him talking like that in front of other kids, but Beth had been there. Anyway, I couldn't wait to tell Nadja! We had been finding less, I thought, to talk about.

Beth and I watched the couples dancing. Two included the bucktoothed Lizzie and the beleaguered Liza. This was why Liza had a nervous laugh, I thought. Then someone was walking toward us. It was the sole other black human being in the volleyball gym, who had just finished his second dance with Nancy Chin. He wiped at his forehead with a handkerchief.

He leaned into Beth. "Wanna dance?"

She stood without smiling.

I decided to wait out the slow songs in the bathroom. As I

crossed the room, someone touched my arm. It was the tall blond boy who had been dancing with Liza earlier. He was a series of squares: head, jaw, shoulders.

He said, "That kid Mike over there really wants to dance with you."

"What?"

"Mike wants to dance with you." He shifted from one foot to the other, raking his fingers through his hair. He jerked his head toward two boys wrestling with each other. Neither of them looked over. Neither of them even secretly tried.

I pushed his hand off me.

"Where are you going? He really wants—"

"You're an asshole," I spat.

"Hey!" I heard him yell behind me.

I felt good stalking away. But then I was in the bathroom with the feeling in my stomach that I'd had when a truck backed slowly into our car one afternoon. My mother sat on the horn, and my father rolled down the window, screaming, *Stop! Stop!*

In the mirror, my hair was a mess of shrinking clumps, and the lipstick was gone. I went into a stall and sat on the top of the toilet. After a couple of minutes some girls walked in, giggling.

"Thea, you in here?" Beth called.

"Yeah. I . . . had to pee really bad."

"So me and Stephanie wanted to know if you danced with that kid," Beth called out. "He's best friends with Mike Harris."

I stayed put. "Who's Mike Harris?"

"God, Thea," said Stephanie.

"Mike Harris is like the cutest guy at Braeford," said Beth.

Stephanie left just as I dragged myself out of the stall. Beth stayed behind and rotated in the mirror with a watchful eye.

"I didn't dance," I said. I considered telling her what had happened, but I knew it wouldn't change the feeling that a truck was backing into my compact. I could only tell Nadja.

"Look at my hair," I wailed.

Beth shrugged. "It's dark out there." Then she leaned over and flipped her head backward, fluffing her own hair.

I decided to change the subject, first glancing under the stalls for shoes. I said, "You know, in third grade, I remember Liza's mom was in the hospital. Supposedly it was for an operation. I wonder if maybe her dad beat her up so bad he put her there."

"Maybe," said Beth. "I think the boring slow songs are over."

We went back out into the dance, where the tall blond boy and his friends pitched their bodies around to "Rock Lobster." I pictured him in a wheelchair.

At 10:30 the lights came up, and even though I was still sweating, I covered myself with my wool cap and coat. When my mother stuck her grinning head in, I practically sprinted into her arms. I almost ran smack into Liza's mother, who looked sad to me. Sad but brave.

"MAYBE THAT OTHER GUY *did* want to dance with you," Nadja said the next night on the phone. I felt like she was pulling rank on me about the dance because she'd already been to four Saint Mary's mixers. Though I usually trusted what she said, this time I knew she was telling me that I didn't know what was going on right in front of me.

"Look, Nadja, *no one* wanted to dance with me. Not even the stupid sellout black guy who was there. And this jerkoff guy who came up to me was just—I mean, he even tried to keep me from walking away. Can you believe that?"

"I believe it, because his friend wanted to dance with you."

I blew out a long gust of air.

"Thea, everything can't be so bad *all* the time. Don't take this the wrong way, but I know things are more interesting when they seem bad. It's just not like that."

We'd had this argument before, and I knew we'd never stop having it as long as we stayed friends, because a lot of things *were* bad. I could just ask my mom about life in the Malcolm X Projects, for example.

With Nadja this time I tried a new tactic: I went silent. Then I added a sniff.

"Are you crying?" she asked.

"No," I said in a small voice.

"Okay, I'm sorry. It's just, what do you want me to tell you? 'Of course that guy was playing a joke on you and his friend'? You're my girl."

"I know," I said. I started to feel a little better, so I told her about Liza's mom. "What do you think about that?" I asked. "I remember thinking that hospital thing was so weird at the time."

"I don't even remember that," said Nadja. "And this girl Beth sounds like a bitch. Why is she talking about people?"

"You and me talked about people all the time," I said.

"We didn't talk about things like that. I mean, did you tell her everything about my mom and her husbands? I mean, if you think it's funny that somebody's dad is beating her mom—"

"Of course not! But I—"

"I have to go," Nadja said. "Sheila's coming here in twenty minutes."

"Please, please don't think I talk about you."

Finally she said, "I know. I really have to go."

It was Saturday night. I curled up in my mom's chair, where I planned to watch *The Love Boat*. I had been reading some other book, but I was feeling so out of sorts that I went up to my room and got *Stranger with My Face*, about the twins, for a third reading.

Back in the chair, I looked over at my mother, who was spread out on the couch wearing her pink house sweats. She snored softly, with *Essence* magazine on her chest. I folded my legs Indian-style and closed my eyes. I thought if I could send my consciousness into space, I would finally see the inside of the Watusi Lounge—where my dad liked to watch Sixers games, then come home to do imitations of the sad men who were always there. I'd spy my brother on South Street, wearing the thin leather jacket he'd cleaned parks all summer to buy. I'd find him hatless and trying not to shiver on the windy October night, leaning against Tower Records, waiting for fine girls to walk by so he could agree with his friends that they were fine.

When I got a little more expert, I could leave the city limits, go out and look for Beth. Was she watching *The Love Boat*? Was she lying on her bed, looking at the latest *Vogue*? Did she have a canopy bed like I'd always wanted? I pictured us in her imaginary room, sprawled on the canopy bed, singing with the Go-Go's. I imagined the two of us sprawled on the canopy bed, quiet. At the same time that my eyes snapped open, the phone rang. My mom reached for it without changing position. "Good evening," she chirped in her extra-proper voice. She handed me the phone and promptly fell back to sleep.

"Hello?" I said.

"Thea, this is Liza."

I only had a second to be surprised, if that.

"Listen up," she said. "Is it true that you were talking shit about my parents?" For once, she neither giggled nor snorted.

There were so many awful things happening in the world. Racist Ronald Reagan was the president of the United States, and the residents of Malcolm X were in dire straits. Ethiopia was starving. Prince was saying we were going to have a nuclear war. It was my father's favorite line in a song: *Mommy, why does everybody have a bomb?* That was how he explained the Cold War to me. That was happening too.

Beth had lied on me, and one of the two most popular girls in my class was furious at the other end of the line.

"Sorry?" I said. I remembered seeing Liza's mom in the bright after-dance light. Her face looked worn under short dark reddish hair, but as the image came back to me, I realized that she had no black eye.

"Sorry you were spreading lies about my parents?"

I could have told her what had happened. Beth was not a good friend to me. But I always felt that she could be. I would protect her reputation, and I would not sacrifice her for Liza van Buren, though it was a sacrifice that twenty-nine out of thirty Barrett girls would have quickly made.

"No, that's not what I meant," I said. "I know it's really bad, but I didn't start that rumor. I was telling Beth something I had heard."

"From who?"

"I feel really bad. I don't want to call anybody a liar."

"Whatever stupid slut you're talking about *is* a liar!" she screamed. Then I heard a door close, and she seemed to get really close to the phone. *"She was talking about my parents!"*

"Okay, I'm sorry, I'm sorry. It was Frances," I said as quietly as I could. My mother knocked her magazine to the floor. My heart jumped, but she continued to snore.

"Frances?"

Liza's voice began sounding far away. Without even trying, I left my body, just like that evil twin. I hovered over the two neat cornrows my mom had done for me that morning while I said very little to her about the dance. I floated past the TV, where I paused to see Ted Lange trapped behind the bar, smiling, the only *Pacific Princess* crew member wearing red instead of white.

If I had really known what I was doing, I would have been able to travel in time as well as space. I would have seen more. Like the ensuing disaster that landed Liza with folded arms, Frances using her regular voice, and me snotting and crying in the middle school head's office. I would have seen that I never mentioned Beth, never gave her up. That Frances never spoke a word to me again unless we were in front of our parents, and that she left Barrett the next year. I would have seen that I would feel responsible for her leaving and that I would feel curiously alone without her until my parents transferred me to public high school, the magnet where my brother went.

I would have seen the surreal conversation I had with Beth on Monday after the dance, when I asked her, in the meekest voice possible, what she had told Liza. She rifled through her locker and said, "Liza shouldn't be talking to you about what I tell her. That's not right at all." Then Stephanie appeared, and they walked to lunch. I trailed behind them in the old halls that were too narrow for three people traveling abreast.

I would have seen Beth's mom at middle school graduation, a young-looking but gaunt woman identified to me as Pakistani, wearing pale face powder. Beth's father was a stepfather. He was old and white, had a lot of bright black hair and a pinched line of a mouth. I would have been able to see how in ninth grade, after I'd left Barrett, Beth invented a boyfriend named Chris who sent her a dancing ape for her birthday.

I SAT, BARELY MOVING, for hours after Liza called. I was still there when my brother came bounding in on a blast of cold air. My mother woke with a start and checked her watch against his midnight curfew.

"I made it," Stephen said.

"Barely," Mom said. My brother looked at me.

"Thea, Thea, Thea," he said happily. "I saw your girl Nadja tonight down on South Street. She was looking *good*." He shook his head as if it were unbearable.

The star of the story

Akousa was dreaming of her twenties. As she went about her daily life, she conducted conversations with people she knew before she got married, before she bought a three-story in West Philadelphia, had a son, got a divorce, kept the house. These people, truth be told, were primarily the different faces of Eduardo "Tu Papí" Negrón, virtuoso trumpet player and *salsero* extraordinaire. Observers might watch her pick over organic red peppers in Real Food or return mystery novels to the library; they might even talk with her as she wove extensions into their hair or sold them a small quantity of pot. All the while they'd be completely unaware that Akousa was dancing with Eduardo between his sets at Eléctrica while the disc jockey spun salsa favorites of the 1970s.

Akousa, née Bette Wilson, had emerged from a prim and hopeful family in Bryn Mawr, Pennsylvania. Both of her parents were teachers. She herself used the pretense of studying to be a teacher at Hunter College to unleash herself on a bigger city than Philadelphia. Those New York years were the fullest four and a half of her life. There were meetings in a basement in Harlem, where Akousa maintained a blackboard list of the revolutionary fallen, and there was the moldy apartment on 145th Street where she came under the tutelage of her terse roommate. In her more generous moods, the roommate, who later went on the lam with some Panthers, taught Akousa to style natural hair and to roll a tight joint, and encouraged her to forget teaching. The girls bonded over their hatred for children.

In New York, Akousa encountered black men from all over the world—West Africa, Jamaica, and England—tall ones who didn't seem hesitant like the colored boys back in the suburbs. There were also Puerto Ricans, an intriguing racial third term of which Bette rarely had caught a glimpse back in Philadelphia.

It was during that time, in Eduardo's arms, that Akousa came into one of her favorite selves, an Afrocentric Lola Falana. She drew herself a grease-pencil mole and refused to wear the same hairstyle two days in a row. She shoplifted bright, beaded slinky things from Macy's and wore strappy sandals in the dead of February. A queen on the dance floor of the African Diaspora, she resided, during the brief time of Eduardo, in the Spanish Caribbean. Akousa danced with all sorts, appreciating dark-skinned Cubans and the tangle of chest hair beneath an unbuttoned shirt. She learned that old men were the lightest on their feet, but she always looked for Eduardo.

"You loved the set, didn't you?" he would ask, smiling what she imagined was the smile of a pimp, greasy and alluring. He kept her whirling with little changes in his right hand, and he worked out the fingering of Colón's trumpet on the back of her one-shouldered red catsuit with his left. The two of them were dangerously hot. But while Akousa escaped to the bathroom to dab her brow with toilet tissue, Eduardo Negrón never broke a sweat.

It was no surprise to Akousa that she tripped around in a trance of memories. She had always been given to fits of nostalgia, everything becoming sweet and sepia-toned the moment it was over. But now she found these moods particularly painful and, worse, clichéd. She was almost fifty, divorced, not rich, and she had been recently dumped by the most inappropriate prospect possible (a what? a street vendor?). When Jill, her best friend and sometime braiding partner, suggested that she might be having a midlife crisis, Akousa narrowed her eyes and said that "authentic people" didn't have those.

Her son, also called Eduardo, who'd recently graduated from college and showed no immediate signs of leaving home, noticed that she had taken all of her Spanish CDs out of their section on the tall, skinny rack and played five of them at a time on "shuffle." The horns and drums started before his alarm clock went off at 7:30 a.m.

"Arriba to you too," Eduardo said on a Monday morning, rubbing gunk out of his eyes. "I could hear that crap all the way up on the third floor."

Akousa was cleaning combs and clips in the deep sink where she washed hair and massaged scalps. "Buenos días a tí también," she said. She sang along to the music with a look of concentration.

Ahora estoy pagando para quererte,
Ay, cariño.

Eduardo cracked open the refrigerator. "Ma, you don't even know what that means."

Akousa waved him off, but regarded him out of the corner of

her eye. He had her flawless dark skin and wore one of his thick, bright sweaters and a pair of soft trousers bought with occasional checks from a father he barely remembered. Eduardo, his mother noted proudly, was the kind of kid who could pull off silver sunglasses on a Monday in February. But he was alarmingly overweight, hiding in the chunky cable of the sweaters and using a leather trench coat to camouflage his ass. She knew because she pulled the same tricks as her body aged and expanded.

Worse than being heavy, as far as Akousa could see, her son was completely alone at the age she remembered as the most thrilling of her life. One thing she wanted for him was to be in love, even if foolishly so.

"I thought you were on a diet, babe," she said more sharply than she meant to, especially since he'd merely put two pieces of bread in the toaster.

"Just toast, Ma. So what's the deal with this music? Never thought I'd miss *Negro Mourning Songs*."

"How'd I let you get so ignorant? That right there is salsa. Just trying to change things up a little."

"I hear that," murmured Eduardo. He spread thin pats of butter on his bread and thought about the bacon-egg sandwich he'd pick up on his way to the office. Then he leaned on the sink, poised to bite, until he caught his mother's glare. He pulled up to the rickety wooden table like a human being.

"You'll miss me when I get my own place," he said.

"Honey, I miss you when you eat over the sink and I'm alone at the table."

They sat together dreaming. Akousa had left the kitchen and found herself in a club called Enter Paradise. There, she watched Eduardo Negrón onstage in a canary-yellow suit singing "Suéltate de Mí." He and the band were in breathtaking syncopation. They could all turn in one movement and stop on a dime: uno, dos, tres, stop, uno, dos, tres, stop. For the finish, they counted in English: one, two, three, because it rhymed with their final *suéltate de mí.* The dancers loved this. It was their favorite part of the night. Akousa's favorite part was when the show ended and she was the only woman allowed backstage into her man's tiny, sour-smelling dressing room. Her son, at twenty-one, was dreaming of his cousin.

EDUARDO WAS IN LOVE. But in practice this consisted of his talent for fantasy and a large, flat sneaker box of remembrances at the top of his closet. He knew that it was age inappropriate to lead a fantasy life with a collection of magazine clippings. But that was just part of the shame. The other part was leading a fantasy life in which one's first cousin was the star.

Then again, not everyone's cousin was Tahira, who could be seen regularly at the newsstands, in a couple of rap videos, and in two low-budget movies that went straight to video. His mother had tried to justify the first film, in which Tahira confusingly played a drag queen.

"Well, I've never seen a woman do that role before," she said. Fifteen minutes into the second one, a graphic depiction of the consequences of marital infidelity, Akousa called her sister to discuss getting Tahira out of Los Angeles.

"The pollution," she said between drags of a joint, "is making her silly, girl."

The essential contents of Eduardo's box, covered with a decoy layer of Playbills and programs, were the history of Tahira's career. There were images of her strutting the runways in Paris and New York. Once she wore a purple tutu. She did ads for Moi Jeans and Santo Vittolini shoes, and picnicked in the park with some "girlfriends," laughing about the new secure protect strip on their maxis.

Then there was her breakthrough, the turning point that precipitated her attempts at acting, a role in a *Men's Monthly* swimsuit issue. Akousa, who used to collect Tahira's pictures, had ceased after these were published.

"Look at this!" she'd said to Eduardo, tossing the magazine at his lap. "I mean, I understand selling a little peek, but this jungle-bunny fantasy is some *bullshit*."

Eduardo thumbed to the pictures. His cousin was set apart from the other girls, not only by her egg-brown face, but also by the fact that she was absent from the beach and pool, where the others lounged in stripes and solids. An oiled-up Tahira crouched and crawled in a makeshift jungle, wearing an erratically ripped leopard-print bikini. In one picture she blended into the greens and browns of drooping coconut trees, her hazel contact lenses the clearest part of her. In this shot, her slim hands covered the parts of the body that *Men's Monthly* could not show: her petite breasts, her hairless crotch. There was no swimsuit.

"That's real bad, Ma," Eduardo said in an earnest voice. He bought his own copy the next day.

For a time, these three pages worn soft with worrying had been Eduardo's most reliable comfort, but also, aside from his wide thighs, his most voluble source of self-loathing. Eventually he put them at the bottom of the pile. It was a truly terrible state of affairs, he decided, when you routinely achieved orgasm by looking at pictures of your cousin that could only be titled—if they were titled—PornogrAfrica.

It wasn't only about jerking off with Tahira, though. It was about tenderness. It was about her first fashion story, a back-to-school spread in *Young Black Miss*, where she wore long skirts and stood near the lockers of the shiniest high school Eduardo had ever seen. And most recently it was all about nostalgia: Tahira at age fourteen, smiling shyly in a light blue V-neck sweater and brown corduroys in a JCPenney catalog. This picture was taken about the time she and Eduardo had fooled around. He wished every day for another chance to be that close to her again, and this time to get it right. He never jerked off while looking at this one, only sometimes touched at the tiny gold heart-shaped locket at her throat, as if he could feel the heat of her neck warming the metal.

EDUARDO MIGHT HAVE EXPLAINED his story this way: life as a chubby, oil-dark boy was hard enough, but his mother had made a parody of him with his own name. At the age of five, she'd sent him into a world of Roberts and Tanyas with the edict "Never let those ignoramuses call you Ed." Eduardo understood that it had to do with the fact that his father, a grim shadow who abandoned them when he was a baby, was called Ed. But if he was at all self-conscious before, it came to Eduardo's attention in fourth grade that it was aesthetically superior to be Puerto Rican with light skin and curly hair (and wasn't El DeBarge fine?). He may as well have been a dark-skinned fat kid named Romeo Billy Dee Williams Valentino.

The roll call of girls he sometimes reviewed, even at the age of twenty-one, went like this.

In the second grade there was tiny Elizabeth Brown, with the massive Afro puffs, who had quietly returned the valentine he'd made her.

In the eighth grade, a loud girl named Lalisa always tried to make Eduardo play "Show me your thing," and then began crying abruptly behind the bleachers when he finally did.

His prom date, a stunningly voluptuous friend named Cara, made out with him briefly in the girls' bathroom just before the dance ended. After they fumbled in the stall—it was an appallingly tight-yet-sexy fit—she had reapplied her lipstick with a businesslike air. The day after graduation she told him she was a lesbian and that the interlude in the girls' room was "just to make sure." She thanked him for being a good friend and hugged him so hard that his belt buckle clawed into his belly. When Eduardo thought about hooking up with her, he recalled that she'd spent most of the ten minutes pawing at his chest and trying to play with his nipples.

In college, he had decided to stop chasing humiliation and focus on other things: getting an internship at a public relations firm and excelling at the mass communication classes at Temple that interested him. This was when Eduardo began using the money his father sent him to patronize the best Big & Tall shops in the city.

"What happened to saving for a car?" his mother said the first time he came home with a heavy plastic garment bag.

"Look, Ma," he said. "Being the prettiest nigger in the city don't come cheap."

"Don't say 'nigger,'" she said. Then she demanded to see

what he'd bought. After that, she was always excited when he came home with new clothes. "Not everybody got it, boy, but you, you *got it*," she'd say.

Regardless of how good he looked in clothes, Eduardo couldn't help but gaze down at his dimpled thighs dripping wet in the shower and think, This is not okay.

Instead of presenting himself as an option to girls when he went to a club or a party with his boys, he assumed the position of commentator. He chatted with women who came around their group; he tried not to flinch when the women compared him to some fat black entertainer. There was the wispy twit of a girl—who had a thing going with the best-looking and most ruthless dude in Eduardo's crew—who told him, "You don't really look like him, but you remind me of Biggie." Her face was bright, as if she had a good idea.

"No disrespect to the dead, but that was one seriously unattractive brother," Eduardo said.

"But there was something about him," she said wistfully.

Maybe, but Eduardo often felt he was suffocating in his own skin. Those times, he made himself remember a couple of days after he had been with Tahira, how she'd glowed in the yellow circle of lamplight in the darkening den of Aunt Cheryl's house. There, because his cousin was fourteen and he was twelve, she nominally babysat him sometimes after school. Somehow she seemed even prettier in the polka-dotted silk headscarf that she wore at home to keep her hair neat for the next day. She regarded him with Bambi-wide brown eyes that afternoon.

"I know you won't tell anybody what happened," she said.

She sat with him, deep in the couch but not too close. She reached over and traced her finger on the back of his hand. She told him that she had started going with a boy named Ronnie at school. After all, Eduardo was her cousin and they couldn't really go together.

"I do love Ronnie a lot, but I trust you, Eduardo," she said.

Just then he'd reached for her, but she stood up.

"No. We can't now," she said.

Eduardo heard the curtness in her voice, but he was sure that he saw anguish in her eyes.

WHILE HER SON noticed the change in her playlist, Akousa made sure he didn't know about her late-night Internet searches on the sticky old computer in the braiding room. These turned up a mention of E. Negrón as the trumpeter of Estrella, "an up-and-coming outfit, mixing the hip-hop sensibility of the South Bronx with the charismatic swagger of the great Latin bands of the '40s," according to the only English-speaking site that had heard of them.

Every week, Akousa visited Tony's Records at Forty-second and Pine to see what was new and strange. This time she went straight to the Latin Explosion section, where she hoped to find E. Negrón on trumpet.

"Hey, Tony, ever heard of Estrella?" she asked.

Tony knew too much about every kind of music for his own good, and he spent a great deal of time fondling his goatee and speechifying about the imminent death of every musical genre that he enjoyed, or used to.

"Yeah, I heard of them," he groaned. "But I never really listened to their record. What you really need to check out are these old Cuban guys, El Gran Combo del Capitalismo Nuevo—"

"But, Tony," Akousa persisted, "does that mean you don't carry their stuff? Estrella's?"

"No. It should be right where you're standing, but I'm telling you on the real . . ."

And it was. Right under Akousa's costume-bejeweled fingers, where she thought she'd just looked. She broke a sweat in the rabbit jacket from Goodwill that she'd draped with a Palestinian scarf. She scanned the CD case. Estrella was too urbane to have their picture on the cover the way some of the groups did. No cheesy smiles, cotton suits, and dripping curlicues of hair for them. The art for their self-titled debut was a mural of a shooting star on a dingy brick wall.

"I mean, a lot of the young kids like Estrella, because they hang out with rappers and the lead guy dabbles on the slam poetry scene, but I like my shit a little more traditional." Tony monologued through the purchase of the album, and Akousa was forced to close the shop door lightly in the middle of one of his sentences.

Waiting for her old Buick to warm up, Akousa took one of the chopsticks she kept in her glove compartment and opened up the CD. The album contained a thin liner including a laconic song list—it made her crazy. No pictures, no shout-outs, no clues. It simply told her that E. Negrón played trumpet on all of the songs and did some backing vocals. Akousa decided to skip her other errands to go home, listen, and see if it was really Eduardo. How she would know, she didn't know. What she would do, she didn't know.

JOHNSON AND ASSOCIATES Public Relations was housed in three swank rooms on the fourteenth floor of a building that also contained an electrolysis center and an emporium of stereo equipment and hollow gold jewelry. Eduardo loved being associated with the office's muted cream walls and the diminutive Stella Johnson, with her unfathomable ambition and relentless array of tailored pantsuits. When he'd begun there as an unpaid intern in college, he recognized it immediately as an antidote to the left-of-center creative blackness he'd learned at his mother's house. Eduardo didn't mind that his job included staving off bill collectors, cold-calling rude potential clients, and dirtying his hands clipping pertinent items from periodicals. He imagined one day inhabiting the best office in a suite like this one, his name linked with the Right events and the Right people.

An added bonus to the job was that he shared the responsibilities of being Stella's valet with the new intern, Suzette, a college senior who did graphic design for a lunch stipend. Eduardo liked to talk to Suzette about his mother's antics (the what? the street vendor?). Once, when downtown with his mother, Eduardo had run into Suzette, and perhaps because Akousa was looking particularly wild, it had been love at first sight for Suzette. Only an artist, Eduardo thought, would be charmed by the tiny twigs of hair sticking out all over his mother's head. "How did she find the courage to be so different?" Suzette had asked him dreamily when she next saw him in the office. An art major in a family of M.B.A.s, Suzette had a vested interest in finding the courage to be different.

"Salsa?" she said when Eduardo tried to explain what Akousa was up to lately. "Oh my God, does she speak Spanish too? Does she dance?"

"Yeah, I think so. All of that." Eduardo didn't actually know. But he felt glamorous in the glow of Suzette's admiration.

"I just want to call her up and *hang* with her," she said.

"Let's not get crazy, babe," said Eduardo, who worried that if she got to know his mother, Suzette would find that Akousa wasn't so great after all—that she was kind of a mess.

"I wanna grow my hair out just so she can braid it."

"Are you trying to stalk my mother?"

"Is anybody going out for my insulin shot?" called Stella from the big double office. She wanted coffee. "Anybody?"

"Anyway," Eduardo continued, "if you had braids swinging down your butt, that man of yours, Jay, excuse me, Jahlove, would drop you so fast—"

"For all you know, I'm not speaking to *Jahlove*," Suzette retorted. She often talked trash about Jay, which gave Eduardo license to do the same, but he heard a new note of exasperation in her voice.

"Dears, I am flatlining in here!"

Suzette and Eduardo did rock, scissors, paper, shoot! to see who would face the wet cold. When Eduardo won, he braced himself and went anyway. Circling the block, he considered Suzette, as he sometimes did. She was thin, flat-chested, and brown-skinned, with a gap-toothed smile and a little Afro. Eduardo admired her hands, imagining that her artistic talent lived in her long, slim fingers.

He supposed that she could like him, though it was always hard to tell if somebody would have the imagination to like him.

Eduardo daydreamed of telling Suzette about Tahira. In addition to her hands, he enjoyed Suzette's sympathetic look. She cocked her head to one side, wrinkled her brow, and smiled. This particular smile was perhaps her best feature.

AKOUSA HAD A WAY of imparting her feelings to the house. Eduardo could often sense if she was irritable, cheerful, or outraged before he saw her face. When he walked in the door that night, he could feel that she was restless, still listening to her new music on the four-foot speakers he'd convinced her to buy. Then he heard a shrillness in her voice as she made a comment to a customer.

"Hey, booby," he heard her call out just as he considered slipping up the living-room stairs to his room. "Come on in here and say hi!"

She was in the braiding room, where she had finished a woman who always got the same cornrow crown. The woman admired her hair in the large wall mirror while Akousa sprawled in the purple love seat. Eduardo noted that she was wielding a water glass half full of something he guessed wasn't juice. His mother was a weed smoker of the greatest loyalty, and alcohol threw her off.

"Ma?" he said, staying in the doorway.

"Look what Miss Naomi brought us! Rhubarb wine!" Akousa said, lifting her glass in a toast to nothing. There was a near-empty bottle on the low table where she kept her portfolio of hair photos and magazines.

"Oh, thanks, Miss Naomi," he said, catching Naomi's eye. She winked.

"She went—where'd you go, girl?"

"Munificent Falls, Ohio."

"You're gonna have to go back and get me more of this," Akousa said, and drained her glass. "I feel good now." She poured another.

Eduardo walked his mother's client to the door.

"You take care of your mom, now," said Miss Naomi, putting on her coat. "I thought she would save a little bit more for later, you know?" Her dimples puckered.

Clutching her glass, Akousa followed Eduardo around the house as if he were going to steal something. When he went upstairs to change out of his good pants, she stood on the landing between her second floor and his attic. "Have a good day?" she called.

Akousa trailed Eduardo back down to the kitchen, where they usually got their own meals, and gave him a full inventory of what was available for dinner, though she knew he liked to eat bowls of raisin bran at night.

Then she followed him to the living room, where he ate in the old leather recliner that he favored. He wanted to turn on the TV.

"Ma, mind turning your music down?"

"Let's just listen to this new one I got. Give it a chance." She jumped up and came back with the CD case for Estrella. Eduardo didn't read Spanish.

All the songs were the same. Exactly the same, Eduardo thought, except for one where a man rapped slowly in accented English. And all the shit sounded so *happy*. Not like the music he'd grown into, seventies soul that took things seriously: the planet, the races, the disco.

"The people, the gente / P'arriba, al frente!" Akousa chanted. He could take it no longer.

"Ma!" snapped Eduardo. "What do you *want?*"

"Okay, okay." She put her glass on the coffee table. "Son, how well do you remember Edward?" she asked.

"My dad?"

She nodded. Eduardo described for his mother a light green kitchen and his father's mustache. But he didn't know if he remembered that from the handful of pictures he had seen.

"Then you wouldn't be too upset if you weren't, say, named after him?" Akousa said shyly.

Eduardo knitted his eyebrows. Then he learned, to the sound track of Estrella and the fumes of rhubarb wine, that he was not named after Edward, but instead for Eduardo "Tu Papí" Negrón. The story he'd always been told was that his parents didn't want him to carry the exact same name as his father, and the Spanish variation was more special.

"Your father left me just after he found that out. I mean, that wasn't why. You might remember we didn't get along too well," she said, rubbing her cheeks with both hands. Then she seemed to wait for Eduardo to nudge the story along. He didn't. She continued.

"Some of my girls from the old days came for dinner and slipped up talking about Eduardo. By that time, you were about two, and I didn't think it was a big deal anyway. But your father said something corny like 'This is the last straw.' Who says that?" She rolled her eyes, picked up her glass, and drained it. Eduardo had seen her this drunk only twice. The most recent time, she'd been dancing around this same room with her street vendor boyfriend, who'd stopped coming by after that.

"Wait. Edward is my father, right? You're not trying to tell me that this other dude was my father?"

"I wish," Akousa mumbled. "No. *Of course* Edward is your father. By the time *Edward* showed up, Eduardo had dropped me like garbage."

Eduardo the younger wanted to go to his room, close the door on this carnival-happy music, and bury himself in the covers. Instead he heard himself ask about Eduardo Negrón.

"You really want to know this?" Akousa asked, but she launched without waiting. "I mean, we were only together for two months at the most, but it was dragged out over a year and a half. And I wasn't the only one. The story was that he had like eight children by five women or something. One night after the show, I was really smelling myself that night, I guess, because I got all bold and asked him, 'Eduardo, how come it can never be just us?' And he looked straight at me, had the nerve to be putting on face powder, and he goes, 'Because that's not enough, morenita. It won't ever be enough.' But then he took me back to the hotel where he stayed and, ha, fucked the shit out of me."

"Ma!" Nauseated, Eduardo squeezed his eyes shut. When he opened them, Akousa was still there.

"I know, baby. I'm sorry, I'm sorry." Her eyes were hazy. They sat for a minute while the CD player clicked and whirled for the next selection.

"I shouldn't have said that. I'm sorry."

Eduardo snarled. "Why would you tell me this crazy shit? What am I supposed to do with it?"

"I don't know . . . maybe you want to start going by 'Edward'?"

"Maybe you could start going by 'Bette.' Shit!"

"Hey, I'm not that drunk. Did you just curse at your mother? Twice?"

Eduardo sighed.

"Look," Akousa started, "it's just—I've just been thinking about those times when I was your age. I was really a good dancer, you know."

There was something poignant, always, beneath the excitement his mother brought to their lives with her clients, boyfriends, phases, music, and memories. The sadness was a repeating bass note under the other noise. Eduardo talked so he wouldn't have to hear the note now.

"Maybe if you'd had less fun back then, you wouldn't be so down about it now. Did you ever think about that?"

"God," Akousa said, cracking a small smile. "You really are *Edward's* child." She got up and reached behind the Bible on the bookshelf, where she kept her rolling papers. "I don't suppose you want—"

"No thank you." Eduardo decided to leave his mother to her evening. On the stairs he stopped and turned to her. "Ma, you'll be okay? You won't get sick or anything?"

"Oh, babe, you are too sweet. He's so sweet," she said to her cigarette.

Tucked into bed in his drafty room, he considered the solace of the shoebox. But he wanted to feel clean, so he tried to get to sleep flipping through a *Black Enterprise* he'd brought home from the office. By the time he'd reached the ads at the back of the magazine, he still didn't feel like sleeping.

Eduardo called Tahira several times a year. She rarely answered her phone, so he usually hung up without leaving a message. He'd wrestle with the impulse for days, all the while planning a script. In the end, with his finger on the trigger, he'd decide that it was okay to keep in touch with your family. They had grown up together.

Eduardo dropped the magazine. He picked up his phone and dialed, calculating the time difference as an afterthought. He tried to recall the game he ran the last time. Her phone rang three times, and his right armpit dripped.

His cousin sounded husky, as if she had been asleep, though there were voices and music in the background.

"Hey, E," she said. "Is Auntie trying to get me?"

"What do you mean?"

"She keeps coming up on my caller ID, but she never leaves a message."

"Oh, I-I don't know," Eduardo stammered (she had caller ID now!), trying to remember his "reason" for calling, his questions about the entertainment business for the public relations firm where he worked. They seemed contrived now as Tahira yawned.

"Is everything okay?" she asked as a reciprocal yawn tugged at Eduardo's jaws.

He gave it free rein, hoping it made him sound nonchalant. "Oh, yeah," he said. "I'm working for this PR firm here in Philly. They do events around here, concerts, book tours, fund-raisers, some stuff in NYC"—he winced at himself—"and I want to keep doing the same type of thing, you know, but I'm wondering if the place for me isn't out there in L.A."

She perked up. "Yeah, I mean it's a lot of white people getting money off black folks in the industry out here. You should definitely come get some. I know some dudes who are trying to start an agency, and I think they're gonna pull it off, but to tell you the truth, I used to deal with one of them and he wasn't shit, and his boy tried to . . ."

Eduardo wondered if she thought about when they were little. Sometimes he knew that she didn't.

"I know it's corny, but E, you gotta follow your dreams," she was saying, and then there was a commotion on the line. Eduardo heard Tahira yell, "Wait up, bitch!" and then, "E, I'm so sorry, I gotta go. I want to talk to you more soon, though. Love to Auntie, okay?"

He managed to beat her hanging up.

There, nothing wrong with that, Eduardo thought. He listened to himself breathe.

THE NEXT MORNING found Akousa cotton-mouthed, headachy, and unprepared for an eleven o'clock customer. She picked up the combs, clips, and oil jars in her braiding room and mused over her conversation with Eduardo. Akousa knew that he didn't need to know the things she had told him. She had only wanted to share her glory days with someone else, which was awful. She punished herself further by thinking of how easily her son went from being justifiably angry to making sure she would be all right.

When she put on water for tea, Akousa noticed the answering machine message light blinking on the kitchen counter. Next to it was the empty wine bottle, making a sticky ring on the white surface. The message was from Eduardo at his office.

"Hey, Ma, I was flipping through the paper, and that group you keep running into the ground, um, Est-er-el-a, they're playing at some club in North Philly next weekend. I'll bring you the ad. Peace."

She was awful, but she was lucky too.

For a week and a half, Akousa encouraged Eduardo and her friend Jill to talk her out of the Estrella show. She knew the real Eduardo Negrón couldn't possibly be there and she would wind up feeling like one of those women in movies about the inner lives of crazy women.

Her son wasn't interested in saving her from herself. "You should get out and have some fun, Ma," he said when she complained that she was too old to be up in the club.

Jill was no help either. "You need to go somewhere and do *something*. I don't like it when you go without a man for too long. It's unseemly," she said.

"I'm not looking for a man."

"Unseemly," repeated Jill.

In preparation for Club Rojo, where she expected she might be the only black woman, Akousa asked Jill to give her micro-braids and leave the ends out as if it were her own hair. Jill plaited in Brown #2 extensions along with the Jet #1 that blended into Akousa's color. This was a style that she and Jill mocked behind the backs of customers who requested it. They called it a Diana Ross. They hated that backstabbing, white-washed Diana Ross.

On the appointed Saturday night, Akousa pulled out the stretchy black scoop-neck dress she wore when she wanted to show off her cleavage. The skirt contained enough material to swirl; it was a dancing dress. After putting it on, she hesitated for a moment, feeling the waistline pinch more than she remembered. Also, she wondered if she should costume herself as an aloof music enthusiast in a sweater and slacks. Tony had said that Estrella was a group of young kids. What if the audience was all young kids? But what if it *was* Eduardo Negrón on trumpet, and she was there, carrying at least a pound for each of the twenty-some years they hadn't seen each other, wearing the cowl-neck that she wore when she wanted to look like someone who paid taxes?

Finally Akousa came down the stairs, coughing in response to her own spicy perfume. She could feel that Eduardo was edgy. She guessed it was because they often spent Saturday nights together, even if she had company. On those nights, they all stared at the TV, watching a mystery on the British cable channel or some melodrama on BET. Sometimes they listened to Akousa's favorite music from when she was a little girl or a teenager or in college: Dionne Warwick, Nina Simone, Fela Kuti. She told him the same stories again and again about the first time she heard this song or that. Eduardo always asked her questions she couldn't answer, about how many copies a record had sold, for instance, or if the artists owned their masters.

Tonight he was in his chair, feet on the attached footrest, flipping channels in the dark. He looked up.

"Where you going? The ho stroll?"

"The things you say to me," she said, shaking her head. "Look, this concert was your idea." Akousa tried to sound stern, but she wondered if she should wear a blazer over the dress or just stay home altogether.

"Wasn't my idea for you to wear that," Eduardo said. "You just finished getting rid of that last underemployed freak. Why don't you take it easy for a minute?"

"Look, maybe if you didn't spend so much time minding my

business, you might have some of your own," Akousa said before she could stop herself.

"Nobody's checkin' for this." Eduardo gestured toward his gut.

"You could lose some of that weight. But good women aren't worried about that. They just want a decent man."

She didn't quite believe this, but she did remember that some time ago, she and Eduardo had run into a cute, skinny sister downtown who worked with him. He had never mentioned her, but Akousa wondered. She walked over to the couch, grabbed his head, and kissed the top of his hair.

"Get off me," he said, patting his fade protectively. "For all you know," he said, making what he thought was a sly smile, "I have a jawn out in the hedges waiting for you to leave."

"Well, could you ask her to cut them? I see your whole 'pretty nigger' thing doesn't include your old chores."

When she kissed his head again, Eduardo thought about asking whose hair she was wearing, but something told him to keep the question to himself.

CLUB ROJO was in a part of North Philadelphia where Akousa had never been. Pulling her boat of a car into an empty space across the street from the place, she remembered going to discos and leaving her winter coat in the trunk. She had a sense memory of shivering outdoors in a thin dress on a thirty-degree night. You couldn't make an entrance in your black wool church coat. Now she was too old to suffer for that kind of folly. She wrapped up tight and saw in the line, to her relief, not only slender, shiny young girls and twenty-something men in leather jackets with pile lining, but older couples with linked arms. She found it moving that the people dressed dazzlingly to step out over broken bottles, to be surrounded by abandoned houses, and to stop for cigarettes at a corner store called the Hole.

Once inside Club Rojo, Akousa checked her coat. *"Gracias,"* she said to the coat-check girl.

"You're welcome," the girl answered.

The club had a flat red carpet that led up to a midsize dance floor. Above the dance floor was a small stage with a red curtain. People on group dates crowded in booths on the side of the room. In Akousa's daydreams, the tables were in front of the stage and she sat in the center a few rows back. She had pictured herself catching Eduardo's eye as he played. Goodbye to that dream.

When she called earlier, she had been told that the band was going to hit the stage around ten-thirty. It was a little after ten when she was settled with a gin and tonic at a table for two. The DJ alternated between short sets of salsa and merengue. It occurred to her that instead of trying to get Jill to talk her out of it, maybe she should have dragged her along. But then she thought it was embarrassing enough to watch herself go though these motions. Akousa concentrated so hard on feeling like a fool that she didn't notice the man appear at her elbow.

"Do you dance?" he asked. He was short, thick, and neatly dressed, with salt-and-pepper hair. Akousa thought he smelled like the darker notes of cinnamon. She pushed aside some of her Jet #1 locks in a coy sweep.

Though she did the Electric Slide at the occasional fundraiser or second wedding, she hadn't danced salsa in years. It came back easily after her first few silent counts to three. They danced well. He made suggestions with his heavy, weathered hands. He twirled her into him, then out, over and over again. Akousa felt the skirt swirling against her calves. Just when she had caught her breath, he dipped her into the final bars of a song. Enjoying a charge that spread outward from the center of her body, she imagined herself as others might see her, the dark woman with swinging hair, glistening with exertion.

The man wiped his face with a handkerchief. Akousa smiled and began moving back toward her seat. "Thank you."

"Where are you going?" he asked.

They danced the next one and the next. There was a double-time merengue that inspired some of the couples to lower themselves toward the floor in a squatting movement. The women poked out their behinds and wagged.

"El Perrito. The little dog," clarified her dance partner with a sheepish smile. "It's a dance." Something about El Perrito moved him to initiate conversation.

"I'm Oscar. I've never seen you here. What's your name?"

"Akousa."

"What?"

"Akousa?"

"Oh," he said, not pronouncing it. The stage curtain yanked up crazily.

"¡Somos Estrella, y ustedes son estrellas también!"

The men on the stage in crisp white guayaberas roared from zero to sixty in seconds. If Oscar was distracted from the conversation, Akousa was distraught. She tried to keep up with her steps while scanning the stage. Then she saw. On trumpet, of course, was a pale lemony kid with a monobrow who couldn't have been born before 1970. It wasn't his fault that she hated him.

She told herself that she'd known it would not be *him*. Still, something about the wiry monster in his place made her legs shaky and tired. She wanted to take a break, but she kept dancing, a familiar sensation. Dancing miserable reminded her of being on the floor with one of those skilled geezers, determinedly not looking across a room at Eduardo Negrón as he snuggled in a booth with some other bitch. Well, Akousa told herself, it didn't matter then and it didn't matter now. She'd never even seen the man in the daytime.

The club was louder, so Oscar leaned into her ear and tickled her with his mustache. "Where are you from?"

She knew that his question was, Why do you know how to dance?

"I used to live in New York a long time ago," she said. "I went to the Latin clubs."

"Eléctrica, Enter Paradise, where else?"

"Calor and Dance Room. You went?" Akousa said, growing interested.

Oscar nodded.

"Where are *you* from?" she asked.

"I'm from Spanish Harlem. But we live in Camden. I mean, I do. Sorry, it used to be we. Still can't quite get used to it, but my wife and I are recently separated."

Before Akousa could offer mechanical condolences, he got even closer to her ear and gripped her harder. "I know you! You used to come around Eduardo Negrón's band." He grinned. It could have been a wonderful, amazing, miraculous surprise, but coming so close on the heels of her disappointment, Akousa felt found out in a way she disliked.

"I did," she said.

"*La Morenita!* Still love salsa, eh?"

"I guess. I haven't spent the last twenty years backstage, if that's what you mean," she snapped.

Oscar's lush eyebrows shot up. "Easy, easy," he said, softly squeezing her biceps. "It's great to see you. Wanna take a rest?"

Akousa darted her eyes toward the stage and allowed Oscar to buy her another gin and tonic. And then another. She told him about her life since the 1970s, her own failed marriage, her son, and her braiding business. He complimented her hair.

Finally, trying not to sound very curious, she asked, "Were you in the band?"

"I followed them around. They stuck me out to patrol the backstage sometimes, remember?" He smiled again, but it evaporated. "I play a little piano, but I just liked the scene."

"I haven't gone dancing in forever," Akousa said, thinking this might establish her as a grown-up. She would have felt even more superior in her cowl-neck. Of course then she wouldn't have had anyone to dance with. "Do you go out a lot?" she asked.

"Well, it fills the time—being alone, you know," Oscar said, looking down at his drink.

Akousa began to feel close to this man, who was a little sleazy, a little pathetic, and a little attractive. She said, "You know you could scoop up any one of these young girls with your dancing. I used to love getting out there with older men back at the clubs. They always knew what they were doing."

Oscar said, "I'm not looking for some young girl. That's the problem with my wife. She acts like she's still twenty. I tell her, 'Look, honey, be glad we don't have to go through that again.' "

"You never lied," Akousa said quietly. She thought about the drive home, the feeling that the house had on a Saturday night when she and Eduardo were there together, alone. Even worse than those thoughts was the image she had of letting herself into the house bearing the same exposed cleavage, the same trashy hairdo that she left with, those weapons of dance-floor war that now mocked her defeat.

"You know—" Oscar began.

Here it comes, she thought.

"You know, I can't believe how much more beautiful you are now than when I knew you before."

"Think it's that easy, huh?"

"No, and especially not with the most beautiful woman here tonight."

"I am beautiful," Akousa said, almost to herself.

Oscar pushed back his chair, stood, and held out his hand to her. Akousa tried to smile. She looked up at Oscar and said, "Please." She meant to sound disgusted. Instead it was a request.

When she went to stand, Akousa realized that she was drunk. She and Oscar made their way outside in awkward movements, their arms linked like the couples she'd seen earlier. Oscar brought her to his old wood-paneled station wagon. When Akousa pretended to balk one last time, he grabbed her hand.

"Ay, morenita, it's too cold for indecision."

The wind whipped at her skirt as if to second him. As Oscar keyed the ignition, Akousa thought briefly about calling her son. He could probably get there somehow and drive her home. She didn't like the thought of seeing him just then, though. She'd been such a mess recently.

With Oscar's hand on her thigh, they rode from North Philadelphia and through the desolate streets of Camden to a cramped apartment with a brown-and-orange carpet. In this place, Akousa had the best sex she'd had in a long while, in a surprisingly soft and sweet-smelling bed with a fake oak headboard. Oscar was firm in his demeanor, placed her this way and that. It felt good to be managed by someone else. Finally, panting, he kissed her cheek and lay next to her. He laughed.

"What are you laughing at?" she asked.

"I don't know," he said. Then he arranged himself so that her head lay on his chest.

She sighed. "I'm going to tell you something."

"Uh-oh."

"Just listen, man. You know the band tonight? I have their record. The cat on trumpet is named is E. Negrón. I thought he might be Eduardo, and that's why I came."

"You don't know what happened to Eduardo?" Oscar said. He suddenly sat up against the headboard, upsetting Akousa's head.

She jerked up as well, trying to see him in the dark. She wanted to turn on the light, but the lamp was on his side. "Did something happen in Puerto Rico?"

"Oh, that." Akousa was sure that Oscar was rolling his eyes. "Eduardo going off to fight for Puerto Rican independence—he never got to Puerto Rico. Eduardo ain't Puerto Rican."

"What?"

"I can't believe you never heard this story. It turned out he had made his whole self up. Turned out he was from Denver. But his dad was in the army, I think, and they had spent some time in Puerto Rico when he was younger. He dropped out of high school and came to New York and wanted to play salsa and didn't think he would get over as a moreno, you know? It was fine for a while, but he had left this white girl out in Denver with two kids, and she caught up with him, blew up his spot."

Akousa's mouth was open, swallowing the dark, so she closed it.

"Yeah, she came to Enter Paradise one night and pushed her way backstage. I don't know how she got those dirty-looking kids into the club, but she did. Eduardo tried to keep playing with the band after that happened, but it was too embarrassing. I mean, he was a great musician, good bandleader, but the guys didn't respect him anymore, lying like that. And he was the main one always making jokes about us Boricuas this, us Boricuas that. I think he went back west."

"What was his real name?" Akousa asked, though she didn't want to.

"Check this out: Reggie Jenkins."

Akousa made a harsh sound that began as a laugh. She lay back down, holding herself. She wanted to be angry with Eduardo, but instead she felt only a pulsing shame. Reggie Jenkins.

Suddenly Oscar switched on the light. "I hope I didn't ruin all your memories," he said.

"I have more memories than that," she said, blinking, and for a moment they sat in bed, knowing that they were strangers.

"Hey, Akousa, you want some water or something?"

"No thanks," she said.

Still, he came back with two glasses, and they drank in silence. Finally they settled under the covers in the dark. In a sleepy voice, Oscar said, "You're wonderful, you know that?"

Too tired to say anything else, Akousa muttered her thanks. Then she drifted off, thinking she was forty-six and a fool, but at least she still had it.

One person who did not agree was Oscar's wife, who had

planned to surprise him by coming home early the next morning from her mother's in Newark and making a big breakfast. When Akousa's eyes flipped open, the first thing she saw was a petite purple-faced woman, who was beautiful even in her stunned fury. The woman stood in the doorway bedroom shaking her head.

"Oscar, no!" she wailed. "No, Papá, no!"

Akousa jumped up and grabbed her dress, her underwear. Ignoring her, the woman pushed on Oscar's shoulders while he tried to pull her down onto the bed. They spoke to each other in Spanish, sounding choked. Akousa did hear the words *negra* and *puta sucia*, but other than that, they seemed to have forgotten her.

In the living room she threw on her coat and steadied her high-heeled feet. The voice of the man who'd talked her into bed rose louder and louder. Her hands were trembling.

She was awake now, remembering the show, the trumpet player, dancing, and Eduardo. Reggie. As she walked and walked, she thought, Why'd it have to be so fucking hard to find a pay phone in the ghetto? Stepping unsteadily around flying paper and the cracks in the sidewalk, she conjured her warm living room, her music, her son, her life as it was.

SOMETIME AFTER TEN on Saturday night, Eduardo stared at an infomercial about a barrette-looking thing that could cut vegetables rapidly. He found such programs comforting. They came on at strange times, for awkward periods (the Veggie Clipper was about seventeen minutes), and gave him a feeling of timelessness. They kept him company while he washed dishes, read magazines, or took Saturday-afternoon naps. But tonight the thought of his forty-some mother out on the town made him turn off the television.

He decided to call Suzette. She was always saying they should hang out. He thought of her the way you might decide to eat leftovers at home when what you really wanted was something made in a clay pot or a brick oven.

"Hello," she said, clearly meaning to sound glum.

"Hey, Suze, it's Eduardo. You get hit by a car or something?"

She said she didn't want to go out. She had, like, no energy. Then she intoned the would-be magic words: "Why don't we just rent a movie?" Wasn't that what every lonely man longed to hear on a Saturday night? Why didn't they just rent a movie, indeed? She said she'd be by in about an hour and a half. Eduardo daydreamed fleetingly that he and Suzette might have the good sense to settle for each other one day.

He stood and stretched, working out nervous energy through the tips of his fingers. He assembled an eclectic group of CDs in the tray in case someone turned on the stereo. Leaving the Estrella CD, he added the sound track to a movie about fifties jazz, a Nina Simone compilation, and a record by Heatwave. He had recently discovered that there was much more to Heatwave than the tired classic "Always and Forever." He loved best one of their slow jams that swelled with strings. He could not hear Johnny Wilder sing *an-gelll* without imagining Tahira's slender neck. Even though Akousa said the song sounded like a nightmare, Eduardo thought of Tahira in the chorus. *'Cause you're the star of a story I love so well / The star of a story I'll always tell.*

He put that track on repeat and walked into the kitchen. He opened the refrigerator and then closed it. He opened and closed it again. He thought about going up to his room for a brief moment, taking out Tahira's pictures, just to calm himself. So he did.

Suzette shuffled in wearing the opposite aspect of what one-on-one movie night should look like. Her hair was on the linty side, and she wore nonmatching college sweats.

"Hey," she said. "I got *Claudine* and this other thing, *Enemy Kin.*" She held one movie in each hand.

"Cool. I never saw either of those." Eduardo busied himself walking back into the kitchen.

Suzette followed. "You never saw *Claudine?*"

"She never saw *me.*"

Suzette barely smiled.

"What's wrong with you?"

She pulled out a chair and sat heavily. "It's just nothing," she said, putting her face in her hand and closing her eyes for an instant.

"Come on. Tell Eduardo everything."

"Hey," she said, suddenly looking impish, "do you have anything to drink?"

"It's really no booze around," said Eduardo. "But I roll the tightest spliff this side of Kingston."

As a rule, Eduardo didn't smoke. He liked to stay clever and airtight. But he took an occasional drag while Suzette got stoned and told him at length about the increasingly irrational demands that Jay "Jahlove," a white reggae DJ, was making upon her. He didn't like her to take too many showers. He said she smelled artificial. He was training himself, with her help and a guide called *Bend Over, Boyfriend,* to be able to accept a whole hand up his rear. It had seemed exotic when it started for Suzette, who had never dated a white guy and previously had only plain sex. Nonetheless, it had started to feel distinctly "just wack."

"But some of that crazy shit was fun," she concluded.

She and Eduardo sat for a moment of silence, as if both of them were longing for the days of crazy fun.

Then she said, "Hey! I don't have anything on you. What's the freakiest thing you've ever done?" With a slight look of embarrassment, she modified herself. "I mean there must be *something*."

Eduardo ignored her equivocation. He felt light and wild. He recalled one of the few times he'd gotten high, a day off from high school when his mother wasn't home. He'd gotten the idea to take some shirts he'd gotten too big for and toss them out the back window. The breeze had been firm but soft that day, catching and floating them. After he grew tired of this, he drifted into a nap and forgot the trees wearing his clothes. Despite the fact that he was nearly seventeen, when Akousa came home, saw the shirts and his red eyes, she'd immediately pulled off her belt. She managed to lash him twice before she collapsed on his bedroom floor in a fit of laughing and sobbing.

"I had sex with three girls at once," Eduardo said. He felt as if he were watching those shirts balloon again.

Suzette swatted his shoulder, shrieking. "What? When did that happen?"

"A long time ago. It was my first experience, really."

Eduardo had told this story a few times to male friends, and he loved doing so. He had been careful in high school because everybody knew somebody who knew everybody else in the Philly public schools. And somebody would know that this thing involved not only a girl named Debra and a girl named Peach but also Eduardo's cousin. He knew some guys might not care; they'd probably had dirty thoughts about their cousins, and they'd understand if they knew who she was. But he had promised Tahira not to tell.

"Yeah, it was kind of crazy. My mom used to work at a hair salon then, and I used to hang out with these older girls after school. They would babysit for me when I was twelve and they were fourteen and fifteen."

"Oh God, is this one of those bogus I-turned-out-the-babysitter-before-I-even-hit-puberty stories?" Suzette crossed her arms.

"Do you want to hear this or not?"

"Yeah, but I hope little Hakim Randall who I used to sit for isn't somewhere telling some X-rated lie about me."

"*Anyway*, these girls always talked about boys, but none of them was allowed to date. So they would just spend the whole time talking about this one and that one, and then also what the nasty girls at school had done. And I'd be getting mad excited, you know? So one day I'm like, 'Why y'all always talkin' about it? Why don't you do something?' "

Eduardo usually told the story with omissions of fact and omissions of nuance, but this was the outright lie he always slipped in. He had not started that afternoon; it had started itself somewhere in the mind of Peach, who talked the most, and mostly about girls who sucked dick. Eduardo was watching *Justice League* and eating cinnamon toast when Peach stood in front of the TV and asked him if he had a girlfriend. Debra and Tahira stood in the doorway.

"No," he said.

"Do you want one?" she pressed.

"No," he said. It was true. The only girl he thought was cute was his cousin, and she couldn't be his girlfriend.

"I want to suck your dick," said Peach. "I need to practice."

Eduardo twisted his face up. "That's nasty."

"You know you want me to."

Tahira and Debra giggled. When Peach took away Eduardo's plate of crumbs and grabbed onto his pants, they laughed even more theatrically and fell into each other.

"Leave him alone," Debra shrieked.

Peach started giving orders. "Don't chicken out now! Get over here and help me. Lay down!" she told Eduardo.

"Get off me!" he yelled, but felt himself growing hard. Some years before, Akousa had told him what to do with it, and that it was okay, but the thought of such intimate maternal advice sometimes made him lie in bed very still, hoping to sleep it off. It never worked.

He told Suzette, whose thin eyebrows arched higher, how Tahira held his arms and Debra sat on his legs. When he tried one last time to sit up, the girls screeched so loud that the upstairs neighbor banged on the floor.

"Shut up!" hissed Peach. He was too tired to push when she tackled him back onto the couch.

"It's not that big," murmured Tahira when Peach finally pulled his penis out of his shorts.

Eduardo couldn't move his arms or legs, and Tahira looked at him with curious eyes. His own eyes were filling with water that he tried not to spill. Peach put her mouth around him and moved her head. It was like nothing he'd ever felt, in a good way, but also painful. She was careless with her teeth. Eduardo felt the scratchy material of his aunt's couch underneath him and looked at the stilled brown-and-brass ceiling fan. He heard Superman end the episode: *"He'll have plenty of time to think about that— behind bars."*

Peach sat up. "I'm tired," she announced, wiping her mouth.

"Let me try," Tahira said, and to Eduardo, "Eduardo, you won't tell nobody, will you?"

Without waiting for an answer, she kissed him deeply, pushing her tongue back. It was his first kiss. He wanted to pull her closer and touch her hair, the way he'd seen it on television, but now Peach had his arms.

Tahira, who tasted like potato chips, kissed him for a long time, licking his chin. Eduardo wanted both to keep kissing her and to wipe off his face. Then she stood and pulled up her skirt.

"We're gonna do it."

"No! What if you get pregnant? We're related. That's—that's illegal!"

"You're such a baby," said Peach. "Don't you want to learn how to do it?"

"Chill out. Just through my panties." Tahira sat on Eduardo, who closed his eyes.

She was wearing a blue corduroy jumper and a thin white turtleneck. She had bangs, shoulder-length hair, and a heart-shaped locket. Eduardo shut up, and his cousin straddled him and rubbed. After about a minute he couldn't take it anymore. Tahira pulled off him and squealed at the stuff trickling down her leg.

Peach's mouth dropped open, and she released his arms. "Ooooooh," gasped Debra. Tahira told Eduardo to move so she could see if he had messed the couch.

"To tell you the truth, that was a little too much to handle," he told Suzette. "I've been a one-woman man ever since."

Suzette looked down at the table, where she had folded her long brown hands. She cleared her throat.

"What's wrong with you?" he asked her.

"Eduardo, that's a terrible story."

"What do you mean? The first time is never great for anybody. But that first orgasm, I mean, you know, the one with somebody else—*kablow!*"

Suzette looked up, her eyes unfocused but still somehow direct. "I mean, Eduardo, they held you down. And they were older than you."

"Yeah, it's true I was scared at first—" he said, but he didn't finish the sentence.

Suzette blinked and cocked her head, but she didn't smile. She looked at him with such a fierce look of sympathy that he forgot to breathe. "I think that's a terrible story," she said.

And Eduardo, who felt as if he had been hiding in his skin for years, hiding and waiting, had finally been found.

SUZETTE COLLECTED THE MOVIES and left around two o'clock. As he shut the front door, Eduardo wondered that his mother wasn't home yet.

Upstairs, he drifted in and out of sleep. He imagined himself disposing of the magazine clippings, shredding them into pieces that would be impossible to put back together. He would rip the pieces so small that even if his mother emptied his wastepaper basket, she would have no idea what had been going on all these years. Of course she wouldn't have guessed anyway. When his mother was his age, she was having real adventures. Shit, she was still out there doing it.

A murky dream woke him, and when he looked at the clock, it was after four. Then he slept dreamlessly.

It felt like only minutes later when the phone rang.

THaT
GOLden
summer

when zuie was thirteen, her mother's best friend brought her back a beautiful dress from Bali. It was a yellow sundress with gold threads woven into it, and its neckline gave her almost-cleavage. The first time she wore it was when her parents took her and her younger sister, Sharon, to a new restaurant near Penn for their first Thai food.

"Well, *that's* grown," said Zuie's father after they were seated and he'd had a chance to study her across the glass-topped table. He had recently begun to notice what she was wearing.

"It's exotic," her mom said with a little smile.

"Yeah, well, anything more *exotic* than that, on a thirteen-year-old, should be illegal," said her father.

"The air-conditioning is freezing in here. Aren't you cold in that?" asked Sharon. The same friend had brought her back a wooden instrument that smelled like rotting fruit.

Most days that summer, Zuie put on the dress and her mother's heaviest hoop earrings and tied her head with an orange scarf in what she imagined to be Gypsy-fashion. She moved around the house, thinking, She moved about the lonely old house. She thought, She watched dust rain in on rays of light.

But she always changed out of the dress before her father came home.

Sharon and Zuie had been to day camp in June, and would go to Girl Scout camp for sleepaway in August. In the middle of the summer, Sharon went to Cape Cod for two weeks with a friend from school. It was good that she left when she did. The week before, she'd come to Zuie with a guilty look, holding Zuie's journal. Zuie could act only so furious, since she had written things in the journal such as "Sharon is so ugly."

Ugly or not, Sharon had managed to make the private school they went to a part of her year-round life. For Zuie, her life during the colder months might as well have been a dream she had every year. This summer she had traded a couple of letters with her friend Jenny Gilder while Jenny was at camp, but then she came back. Zuie felt stupid writing letters to someone in the same area code.

The one place Zuie went was the library. Each summer her mother made her join the Vacation Reading Club, with its absurd weekly themes, like animals and the future.

"It'll be good for you to meet some kids with busy imaginations like yours," her mother had said, but Zuie's was the only posted Summer Reading Chart with any books listed. At the end of August the library mailed her a certificate and canceled the awards ceremony.

Zuie wanted someone from school to have another thing like Jenny's end-of-the-year pool party in Paoli. She had worn her new blue bikini, but she didn't swim that day. Boys were there, so she had to keep her hair dry. This was the party where Heidi Smalls had gone off into the trees behind the Gilders' massive house with a guy named Sean. She came back and reported to

Zuie and Jenny that he tried to lick her teeth. Without thinking, Zuie gave her own front teeth a cleansing lick. Heidi saw.

"Are you cleaning your teeth off in case somebody tries to kiss *you*?"

"You think that bacteria swap was kissing?" Zuie retorted.

Jenny giggled, but then Heidi glared at her, and Jenny looked as if she wanted to grab her laugh back. Zuie knew, though she tried not to think about it, that Jenny was better friends with Heidi.

"Whatever you say, Zuie," said Heidi.

Zuie found it hard to keep her eyes off a boy at the party called Alex Silt, who had curly dark hair and red cheeks. While Zuie nibbled at cantaloupe and dipped her big toe in the cold water, she tried to hover near him just in case lightning struck and they wound up behind the Gilders' house licking each other's teeth. Alex seemed not to notice her, but not for the usual reasons of her being black and plain, she thought. While guys like Sean posed poolside, running their hands through their hair, trying to see who was watching them, Alex was too busy for girls. He executed cannonballs, flipped burgers on the grill, and teased the Gilders' ancient chocolate lab. Alex climbed dripping out of the pool, leaned over the dog, and shook his wet head. The dog licked his side with a wounded look, and Alex laughed. Zuie thought she was the only one watching until she locked eyes with a smirking Heidi. Zuie smirked right back.

"I am dying for him," she murmured to Jenny later as they reclined by the pool, rubbing their goose bumps in the not-quite-summer air.

Jenny made a face.

"What?" Zuie said.

"He has a huge nose," Jenny said. "He could snort up all the water in the pool." Jenny's parents had told her, without being asked, that she could get a nose job when she turned sixteen.

"Well, that's your opinion," Zuie said.

Later that summer, Zuie thought about the party while she watched TV shows from the 1960s where housewives constantly offered coffee to guests and husbands. She thought about it when she listened to the rock station on her clock radio. She never missed the four o'clock countdown of the most requested songs of the day. Her favorite was "She's Waiting," by Eric Clapton. Zuie sang along into her window fan, dreaming up Alex Silt. First she could only picture him at the pool, shaking his wet hair or hitting the water. Then she added a scene where he folded her into his arms under the trees. Finally she imagined that he walked into the pool house, surprising her as she changed out of her suit. Naked kissing ensued.

In real life, she tried on the yellow dress, tied her head, drank iced tea, and looked out the window. Neighborhood kids she didn't know sat on row-house steps, jumped rope, and danced through the spray of the fire hydrant. Especially at night Zuie listened to their cries and the wet motors of air conditioners. The street was yellow in the morning, gold around four o'clock, and, later, a wet blue black.

DURING SHARON'S SECOND WEEK AWAY, Zuie felt she needed to talk to someone about Alex Silt, so she called Jenny. Jenny's mother said she'd be back in half an hour from a tennis lesson. Thirty minutes later, Zuie was so afraid that she might miss the call that when she went to pee, she ran back to the couch without washing her hands.

Two hours after that, Zuie was so discouraged that she took a nap. She was on the edge of a sweaty sleep when she heard the phone ring. She ran into her parents' room and grabbed it off the hook.

"Hello," she panted.

"Hello, is um, Zuie there?" asked a voice: adolescent, white, male. The background was very quiet, as if the caller was in a small, empty room.

Zuie's mind flipped through an imaginary phone book of people who might call her, but came up blank. *Unless.*

She tried to slow her breathing. "Who is this?"

"Is Zuie there?" the voice asked again.

"Seriously, who's calling?"

She tried to remember Alex Silt's voice and match it up with the voice on the phone. She could see him on the other end of the line, blushing furiously under a dark halo of curls. How did he get her number? Why wouldn't he say who it was? Why was he calling her now?

He hung up.

Zuie felt the pulse in her wrist. She could barely sit still for her afternoon shows. She stormed into the kitchen during commercials and ate huge handfuls of pretzels. Twice at dinner, where she barely touched a perfectly golden piece of fried catfish, her dad told her to stop jiggling her leg.

"Are you on some kind of uppers?" he asked with an alarmed look when she started up again.

"Gary?"

"Kidding, Alicia," he said. "Just kidding."

It wasn't until after midnight, as Zuie lay awake, that she remembered that she hadn't heard from Jenny. This she recalled in the middle of a prayer to the ceiling that he would call back, that whoever it was would call back.

He didn't that night or for the next couple of days, as far as Zuie knew, anyhow. She couldn't be absolutely sure, because her parents hogged the phone in the evenings. Her dad conducted business briefly (though not briefly enough) on the kitchen wall phone with his eighty-six-year-old mother. Zuie's mom was the real problem. She favored long chats sitting on the den couch with her feet up. One night she called Zuie's grandmother, and the two of them discussed a chicken recipe, her grandmother's foot doctor, the cover of *Jet* magazine, and Uncle Eric's credit-card debt. By the time the conversation turned to the inscrutability of God's ways, Zuie imagined herself going upstairs to eat an entire bottle of Tylenol and lying down on the bathroom rug next to a note that said, "Was it worth it?"

"You sure do talk a lot," Zuie said when her mother hung up.

Her mother arched an eyebrow. "You have all day to make calls. Anyway, it's my phone."

"Who said I wanted to use it?" said Zuie. She folded her arms, and her mother looked confused.

"What's wrong with you? Before you know it, it'll be September, and you'll be complaining about school. If I were you, I'd find a way to have fun. Did you read your book this week?"

"It's about rabbits!" Zuie yelled.

Just then her dad walked in from the kitchen with his nightly bowl of fudge ripple. "Who is she yelling at?" he asked.

The next day, Zuie put on the yellow dress. She called her

mother and told her she was going to the library. She walked around the corner and exchanged her book for an illustrated history of New York sewer rats. Then she broke the rules and continued up Fifty-second toward Market Street. She lingered with vendors on the crowded strip while they ignored her, loudly bartering with adults over the music that pounded from store speakers. She thought about stealing a purple scarf woven with silver thread that looked like her dress. But of course you wouldn't, she thought with disgust.

Zuie inhaled the sweet chemical rubber in the sneaker store, let the beauty supply owner follow her up and down the two cramped aisles, and picked over the crappy T-shirts and socks in a huge discount warehouse. She bought herself an unappealing flat cookie from the flyspecked bakery. At the end of the commercial strip, Zuie stood at the grimy El-stop stairs and considered riding to Thirtieth Street, switching to a suburban line, and going out to the school. She suddenly yearned to see its rolling fields and iron gates.

"Hackman, hackman," called out the illegal cabbies under the tracks. Zuie's dad had pointed them out to her once, and now when she saw them she always wondered where you'd wind up if you got into their cars.

Just off Fifty-second Street was a store called BB Jones, where blouses cost seventy dollars. "Where the hell do they think they are?" Zuie's mom would always ask. The sidewalk outside of the store was just as gum-pocked as the rest of the block, and the vendor there sold batteries and broken toys. Zuie stood erect and walked in.

"How can I help you?" asked the woman at the counter as soon as the chiming door clicked shut. She was a beige color, with drawn-on brows and a thin smile that petered out before it reached her eyes. She looked at Zuie's grease-and-chocolate-smudged cookie bag.

"No—I just . . . ," said Zuie, and then she backed out of the store and walked home, stopping only to throw out the cookie.

She was on the porch of her house, pulling at her key chain, when she thought she heard someone yell "Hey!" She paused and then went ahead and put the key in the door.

"In the yellow!"

Zuie turned slowly to see a big, old-looking metallic gold car idling in the middle of the street. The boy in the passenger seat called out to her.

"Miss! Please, wait!"

Still clutching *Kings of the Underground,* Zuie managed to cross her arms. She looked down at the boy. "What?"

He stepped out of the car in what seemed like an unfolding. Once he was standing, Zuie could see that he was lanky and tall, with light brown eyes and skin the color of honey. Alex Silt was a boy. This was a man.

"Don't be like that, miss. I just wanted to say hi." He wore a frustrated expression, which pleased Zuie. Her actions meant something to him.

"Hi," she said.

"Hi," he said. He looked down the street this way and then that. "So what's your name?"

Denise, thought Zuie. She said, "Zuie."

"I can't hear you all the way down here," he said, cupping his ear with a squint.

"Zuie!" she yelled.

"My name is Earl. That's corny, right?"

"A little," Zuie said, biting her lip.

Earl was already pretty, but his smile changed his face, and the change did something to Zuie.

"Go on, laugh it up," he said. Then he turned back toward the car. "See this, Jamar? This young lady is laughing at my name. Now, is that nice?"

Jamar said something that Zuie didn't hear. Earl turned back to her. "Zuie, I wanted to ask you a question."

"Ask it," she said. She liked the sound of that: *Ask it.*

"You got a man?" Earl half closed his eyes and grimaced, as if to shield himself from the answer.

Yes, thought Zuie. She said, "No."

"That's what I'm talking about! Now I got another question." He beckoned her with his finger. "Come down here, girl. Let's talk like people."

"What?" Zuie said, smiling and descending. He wore a dark green T-shirt that matched his spotless white Adidas with green stripes. Still, she would go no farther than the bottom step.

Earl rolled his eyes with a grin. "You wanna get something to eat with us? We goin' to Friday's out City Line."

"I can't get in your car," Zuie said.

Earl frowned.

Zuie would always remember that day clearly. She would remember Earl's face, aged through the decades, if she saw him on the street tomorrow. She would remember that she was playing with *The Philadelphia Tribune*, still in its plastic bag, with her toe, and that a car alarm went off for a few seconds. The thing she buried under layers of memories, so far down that she couldn't find it again, is what she said to invite the two men into her parents' home. She might have offered them coffee.

Earl did not seem very interested. "Sure you don't wanna hit Friday's?"

"I can't," she said.

He took her hand between both of his. Though his fingers were long and neat, the word *paws* popped into her head. Earl looked her up and down in a way that made her feel a series of points pricking her thighs.

"I'ma see what Jamar says. He might want a beverage before we move on."

Earl gave back her hand, and Zuie stood there while he returned to the car. He leaned in and spoke in a low voice. Suddenly he stepped aside, and Zuie was facing Jamar. Then Earl blocked the way again and the men had more words.

Earl stood back up, his golden face flushed. His smile was gone. "How old are you, Zuie?"

"Sixteen," she said, finally able to lie.

"For real?" He perked back up, but Jamar revved the car.

"Well, later, I guess," Earl said, sounding sad. "Nice meeting you."

The car squealed down the street, and Zuie saw Jamar's hand fly out and make contact with Earl's head. Zuie noticed that they had New Jersey license plates, and she imagined they were headed for the ocean.

"Can't Get There from Here" by REM was the new song at the top of the countdown. Zuie sang it into her window fan. *"I've been there I know the way."*

FOR THE FIRST COUPLE OF DAYS after Sharon got back, she and Zuie were friends. Sharon, whose nose was peeling, taught Zuie bid whist. Zuie told Sharon about Jamar and Earl. Then Sharon started harping on the journal again. Once, as they walked around the corner for water ice, Sharon suddenly said, "You know, Zuie, we don't even look all that different."

One night, the girls' parents came home later than usual because they had gone to an emergency block meeting. Two teenage girls from the neighborhood were missing. Zuie's parents had a stack of flyers. Neither of the girls looked familiar to Zuie, but she wondered if she'd heard their voices among the others at night, screaming the way girls did when they were having fun. At dinner, Zuie's father asked if she and Sharon had seen anything suspicious, if any weirdos tried to talk to them.

"Zuie talked to some guys the other day," Sharon said, looking nonchalant.

Zuie choked on her fruit punch. She thought she and her sister had been having a good day!

"What boys?" Zuie's mother asked.

"Just some boys," said Zuie.

"Zuie, this isn't a joke," said her father. "These folks haven't seen their girls in weeks." Sharon looked deeply involved in making a tuna sandwich with two saltines.

"I'm not being funny. It was these two guys in a gold car. It was a Cadillac or something. They spoke to me first."

"Where was this?" her mother asked in a calm voice.

Zuie's father rubbed his temples and inhaled loudly.

Zuie knew this part was wrong. "They stopped me on my way into the house."

That was it.

"What?" screamed Zuie's dad. "What?" He slammed his hand on the table right near Zuie. Punch jumped up from her glass.

Her mother sometimes called her father Scary Gary, but this didn't make Zuie feel less frightened just now.

"You were entertaining strange men in front of our house? Is that what you're telling me, Zuie? Is this how you reward us for letting you stay home and ride the bus by yourself? After all these years—thirteen years—of us telling you not to talk to people we don't know, you stood on the porch talking to some men who could have forced their way into our house and stolen everything, or pulled you into their car and *taken you somewhere?*"

Zuie looked curiously at her dad, who punctuated his words with an actual jump off the ground. It occurred to her that he loved her. He left the room, went upstairs, and slammed a door. Her mother stared at the spot where he had been. Zuie was pleased to see Sharon's sandwich fall apart before it reached her mouth.

After dinner, Sharon tied up the phone line, reliving Cape Cod moments with her friend. Zuie went to her room and read about rats. On a long list of things rats could chew through, including bricks, the author had included "love letters."

Zuie's mom came in and sat on the bed. She arched her eyebrow. "I don't even need to tell you this, right?"

Zuie shook her head slowly.

"I will anyway. You are not to speak to strange men."

"They were just boys," Zuie said because she couldn't help it.

Her mom didn't get angry. "Zuie. Not to scare you unnecessarily, but even with your imagination you can't imagine the things that men do to little girls."

Zuie pulled the sheet closer to her face and gave enough assurances to make her mother leave the room. What she wanted to say was, "For once, they wanted to do it to me. To me!" But when her mother was gone, Zuie couldn't push her thoughts further than the man holding her one hand with his two. Each time she tried, the whole thing fell apart, and she stood there in her yellow dress watching the gold car drive away.

party on
vorhees!

sɑrɑh mOrris never would have talked to Vetta McCormick if they hadn't been assigned seats together in sixth-period biology. Nor would she have gone out of her way to make friends with the girl, who stirred up a cloud of snickering whispers wherever she went. However, a few weeks into tenth grade, Vetta asked Sarah for her number, and with an inward shrug, Sarah gave it to her. So it was that she found herself standing next to Vetta in a cavernous room on the second floor of Houston Hall at a Penn party. Sarah's younger sister, Grace, always anxious about the figure she cut socially, was clearly embarrassed by this new addition to their number. She disappeared in the direction of the bathroom as soon as they were safely inside the building.

The dark room was filled with boys in loose, neat jeans and patterned silky shirts, girls in colorful turtlenecks, overblouses, and denim skirts. Everyone had complicated hair. The DJ played Brand Nubian, X-Clan, Queen Latifah, De La Soul, and the Jungle Brothers' "I'll House You." When that came on, the crowd clapped out a layered rhythm. Some girls got housed.

Sarah and Vetta moved at a distance from each other so it was clear that they weren't dancing together. A boy walked up and began talking to Vetta.

"Oh, I'm all mixed up," Sarah heard Vetta tell him. "Puerto Rican, Irish . . ." She trailed off.

"Uh-huh," said the guy with a glazed expression, evident even in the darkness.

"I'm also Native American," she added. Vetta was black, with tan-colored pimply skin and full lips that she painted magenta. She was bottom-heavy, and she wore an obvious hair weave back in a ponytail. Dry-looking wisps dangled on the sides of her face. This was 1990, before weaves were everywhere.

After the guy had walked away, Vetta waved the space in front of her nose. "Phew!" she said. "Halitosis Jones!"

Sarah laughed. "Too bad. His cardigan matched his purple paisley shirt so perfectly." She was only half joking. He had looked quite nice.

"I don't think a guy should look so neat," said Vetta. "I think a guy should be kind of a badass, not like a drug-dealer badass, but like James Dean. Don't you think so? What were the guys like at your old school? I bet they were all named Heatherington Wellington."

"It was all girls."

"I know, silly!" Vetta pushed Sarah's shoulder. "But don't all those fancy places hook up with a boys' school so you have people to date?"

Sarah said, "The black girls didn't date."

Sarah could see that Grace had returned from the bathroom. She watched her slink deliberately past a throng of oblivious purple-and-gold-clad Omegas, who Sarah knew would eventually step through the room in a syncopated line, barking. Then

Grace went timidly—almost on tiptoes—up to Central High's student body president, Veroniqua Hollings, initiated a brief exchange, and skittered away. When Grace vanished from her line of vision, Sarah knew where she was.

"This is a cool party," said Vetta. "You go to these a lot? How do you find out about them?"

"This girl Leelee in my homeroom tells me when one is happening." When she feels nice and nobody cool is around, Sarah didn't say. Except for Leelee, Sarah's friends at Central were a sad, multiracial crew of misanthropes who ate lunch together and never traded numbers. There was RJ, a ponytailed Arab boy who only liked to talk about his unfunny zine; an acne-scarred white kid from the Northeast who collected gun magazines; and his sarcastic Vietnamese girlfriend, who charmingly called Sarah Miss S. This year they had been joined by Georgy, a Jamaican boy with a genius IQ whose lips moved silently as he played chess games in his head.

Vetta looked around the room with a sigh. "College is so eclectic. I think people like us'll really rule in college," she said, almost to herself.

Sarah didn't ask, *People like who?*

"So where's your sister? Diving for lost treasure in the can?"

They moved toward the strobe-lit center of the room in search of Grace. There, dancers jumped into the air, challenging each other. Two guys who had been throwing themselves about with ever more aggression made peace by doing the Kid 'N Play. They each linked one foot and hopped in a tight round. Usually Grace hovered near the circle, staring the dancers down with a hunger so plain that it hurt Sarah. Tonight she was there, wearing a small smile for a short, solid-looking boy who stood close to her. Like the boys who usually interested Grace, he looked as if he had dropped in from the set of another movie in his puffy winter jacket and glaring white Adidas.

"Like oh my God, it's Grace!" Vetta said. "Grace, like, what's up?"

Grace's smile fled. "Hey."

"Like, hey."

After frowning slightly at Vetta, the guy looked at Sarah. He had large, deep-set eyes and thick lashes. She had the sensation of being pulled down into his eyes, and she stepped back.

"I'ma check out my man over there," he said, excusing himself.

Grace patted at her hair and looked after him.

"He wasn't bad-looking," said Vetta.

"Who was that?" Sarah asked Grace.

"Some jawn."

"He ask you to dance?"

Grace shook her head and glared at Vetta, who glanced off in the distance for her next wisecrack.

A guy with short, neat dreadlocks and a leather Africa medallion asked Sarah to dance. He looked cool until he began to writhe, sway, and generally do a modern dance routine; she tried to stay out of his way. Someone tapped her on the shoulder. It was a smirking Leelee, slithering by with one of the Omegas.

When the girls emerged from the building at twelve-thirty, Sarah and Grace's mother, who often ferried them around at night, was double-parked in front of the broad steps. The car was filled with her perfume, and she wore her fur-collared coat.

Usually she'd say, "So who was there?" and "Any fine brothers?" and "How was the DJ?" This time she barely got to ask her questions, because Vetta began doing impressions of the Central kids they'd run into that night. She seemed especially to enjoy her version of Veroniqua's shrill, lisping voice.

"She sure can talk," Mrs. Morris said after they had dropped Vetta off.

"I can't tell if she's crazy or retarded," said Grace.

"Look, just because she has a weave," Sarah said, feeling traitorous. She did think Vetta's hair was awful, but you can't bring the dead weight and then criticize the dead weight.

"Sarah, you're lucky I let you go out with that child. You know I don't allow fake hair in the Morris car," said Mrs. Morris.

The next Friday, on the gray, jangling El ride home from school, Sarah mentioned to Grace that Vetta would come out with them again that night.

"Does she have to?" Grace asked.

"What's it to you? Last week you tried to hide in the bathroom for the whole party."

"I didn't need everybody in the world to know I came with her. I heard Veroniqua Hollings and them talking about her at school."

"Yeah, saying what?"

"She thinks she's white."

"That isn't even half of what she thinks."

"Well maybe I'll just stay home tonight," Grace said.

They both knew that she would go. If the girls stayed home while their parents carried on their raucous, adults-only pinochle game or went to a cabaret, Grace sat with a mirror on her lap, shedding her split ends on the cream-colored sofa, using two different sizes of hot curler to style her hair like Veroniqua's. The girls watched nauseatingly sweet sitcoms that left them feeling lost and soiled. Most haunting was the one with that black child actor in suspenders, the iconic nerd, who as he grew older had to pitch his voice to painful heights.

Sometimes they showed up somewhere expecting a party, and it turned out that there was nothing. Since it was Sarah who usually heard about the parties, she always felt guilty. When the tip failed, she let three people down. There was herself. There was Grace, who plagued Sarah with tragic eyes during commercials. Then there was their mother.

According to Aletha Morris, the sixties had basically been one long, red-lit, magical basement party, where horny boys dressed like Smokey Robinson asked "Can I stand a chance?" Then came the 1970s, when she blossomed an Afro and slunk around in bell-bottoms to the sound of the wah-wah pedal. This was when she teamed up with Carl Morris, who alone stood a chance, and they stormed their campus in nowhere Pennsylvania with the funky style of black righteousness. But even while Carl and Aletha studied Marxism and occupied buildings upstate, Fridays belonged to the city and the parties.

"We could always find a house party. My two very best girl-friends picked me up Friday night, and I'd sniff the air and just tell 'em which direction."

To which Grace snapped one night as they drove home from a dark and empty Houston Hall, "Well, you and your very best girlfriends didn't get all messed up going to some white school in the suburbs."

"But you were so popular there, Gracegirl. You loved it."

Grace folded her arms and stared at the sidewalks flying by.

The silence in the car became so thick that Sarah had to open a window.

ONE WARM FALL EVENING, Sarah, Grace, and Vetta wandered in and out of the stores on South Street. It had been three weeks since the first party. They'd gone to one other and one bust. Now Sarah and her sister listened to Vetta generate ideas for her talk show. In fact, ten years later, Vetta would occupy center chair on a poorly lit local program called *Philadelphia Views*, but that night she described *The Vetta Hour*, where she would tell off school dropouts, twelve-year-old sluts, celebrities on drugs, and people like her mother who collected disability because they were too fat to move. Of course she would also dedicate a show to the troubles of mixed kids.

"Take me, for example. I don't talk about my heritage that much, because people think I'm trying to brag or something."

Grace, who rarely addressed Vetta directly, said, "You talk about it every day."

"I don't even talk to you every day, Grace."

"Yeah, but every time we do talk, it's all about how you're this and that and everything but black. You are a black girl, Vetta."

"Guys?" said Sarah, but she didn't really want them to stop talking.

Vetta only said, "Grace, you don't have to tell me that."

Grace narrowed her eyes and walked ahead.

"Shorty! Shorty in the red cap!" called a male voice.

Hatless Vetta made the mistake of turning before Grace, whose red cap perched atop her perfect hair.

"Not you, mophead!" called another.

Vetta cursed the boys in broken Spanish.

"Girl, you ain't Puerto Rican!"

But that day she was, with her messy hair sprayed up PR-style and her eyes heavily ringed in black. The guys flagged her with their skinny arms, and a four-finger ring glinted in the street-light. Vetta rattled off more Spanish, but ended with the phrase *fugly motherfucking pussies*, which she spat with such force that Sarah shuddered.

"Vetta?" Sarah said.

"What did you say?" said the ringleader.

It was only because some flyer girls walked by that his friends were able to refocus his attention.

"Maybe we should go home before Vetta gets us stabbed," said Grace, furiously finger-combing the back of her hair, her eyes wide with horror.

"You scared of those skinny punks?" said Vetta. "You should see the hard rocks on my block."

"Yeah, right," Grace muttered.

Later, Grace and Sarah gathered in the TV room at their father's excited request for a late movie showing of *Black Caesar*. Aletha painted her nails, and Carl sang along with the James Brown sound track, making up the words he couldn't remember. Grace complained to their parents, especially their mother, about Vetta.

"And then *she* turned around, even though it was obvious he was talking to *me*, and then she started trying to speak Spanish. But excuse me, it didn't even sound like Spanish, which I've been taking since the *sixth* grade."

"Gracegirl," said Mr. Morris, "it's true that she sounds a little"—and then he made a two-tone whistling noise—"but the question is, why are you talking through the greatest movie of all time?"

"We've seen this three times," said Sarah.

Mrs. Morris managed to look concerned while blowing her lilac-tipped fingers. "Well, who are her friends at school?"

"I don't know. I don't speak to her at school," said Grace.

Mrs. Morris laughed. "I don't know if that's right."

"You don't speak to the sister at school?" asked Mr. Morris during a commercial. "That sounds a little uptight. What are you so uptight about?"

"Everything!" yelled Sarah, and threw up her hands as if cheering. A memory flashed by of Grace coming home in tears from the first day of sixth grade back at the private school. It seemed that everyone had agreed over the summer that the longer gray kilt, not the short blue one, was in, and she had proudly worn her skimpiest blue kilt.

Now Sarah's entire family glared at her. Even Black Caesar, thwarted as he clawed his way to the top, glared.

The next Friday night, they almost didn't make it out.

After school, Grace played with her hair and Sarah read *Sister Carrie*. When the phone rang, Sarah picked it up and heard a male voice ask for Grace.

Grace said, "I wasn't sayin' nuffin."

And she said, "Das jus stupitt."

And, "Why you gotta be like dat?"

When she hung up, Sarah threw her book aside. "What was that?"

The lamp under which Grace sat made her hair shine while it hooded her eyes. "Look, I don't feel like it," she answered.

"I mean it would be one thing if you *actually* talked like that,"

Sarah said, thinking of her father, who pronounced the *l* in *salmon*.

"What do you want from me, Sarah? You think it's fly to sound like a white girl? Or maybe you think I should get a hair weave and start telling everybody I'm Indian?"

"At least Vetta knows who she is."

"We all do—a freak."

Sarah picked up her book and put her feet back up on the coffee table. Then she yawned.

Grace said, "Well, maybe if you stopped hanging with her and that dork crew, people wouldn't be calling you Auntie Tom."

Sarah got up, walked over to her sister, and messed her hair. Grace stood and pushed Sarah's face, hurting her nose. The girls scratched, pulled, and finally clung to each other.

"Get off me!" yelled Grace.

"You get off!"

Sarah shoved Grace so hard that she fell and hit her head on the side of the coffee table. She touched the spot on her forehead. Sarah covered her mouth and whimpered.

The sound of a truck barreling past the house cut the day in half. Now it was After.

Grace said, "Shit, what time is it?" looking around wildly for a clock.

The last time the girls had fought, their father had pulled them apart, his fingernails digging into their arms, threatening that if it happened again, someone would have to call Child Services on him. Sarah wrapped ice in a paper towel and pressed it lightly to her sister's forehead. They sat facing each other on the drafty hardwood floor. Their parents wouldn't be home for at least an hour and a half.

"You fight like a girl," said Grace. "It's a good thing I *don't* have a weave. We'd be sweeping it up."

"Vetta would probably look better after a fight."

Minutes later, Grace and Sarah had rearranged themselves as they'd been before the phone rang. But Sarah found herself reading the same sentence again and again.

"Hey, Grace," she finally asked. "Who calls me Auntie Tom?"

"I don't know," Grace said. Then she laughed almost long enough to break the peace.

Vetta called a few hours later. She'd heard from Gloria Torres about something in the Puerto Rican part of North Philly. "I need to party with my *gente* for a change," she told Sarah.

Sarah said, "Will the *gente* of Dublin be there too?" She covered the phone when Vetta started babbling a response.

"Grace, you wanna go to a house party with Puerto Ricans in North Philly?"

Because their parents were in the kitchen, Grace touched her wounded forehead and locked her sister's eyes with her own.

I'm sorry, Sarah mouthed.

"There's not going to be a bunch of white people?" asked Grace.

"Unless you think Puerto Ricans are white."

"Sarah, I swear this is the last time I go out with her."

"A house party?" Mrs. Morris appeared in the doorway squealing, fists clenched for dancing.

"North Philly, huh?" Mr. Morris boomed from the kitchen. "What is it—at a crack house? I'm driving out there with you."

In the car, Aletha said, "Everybody talk now. Because when Vetta gets in, your talking part of the night is over."

"Just this last time," Grace repeated in a low voice for Sarah.

About forty minutes later, when they arrived at the address Vetta had given, Mrs. Morris was dubious. "Whoever heard of a house party at a community center?"

Sarah, Grace, and Vetta walked into the high-ceilinged building while Mr. and Mrs. Morris waited at the curb for the okay to leave.

They trudged slowly in their colored sneakers and stylishly ripped jeans past chatting girls in taffeta gowns. The room at the end of the entrance hall poured out Spanish music. Even Vetta was quiet. When questioned later, she admitted that perhaps Gloria Torres had not actually *invited* her to Mildred Ramos's *quinceañera*, a dressy affair involving a sheet cake and adults of various generations. Sarah also thought it was a possibility that Vetta, despite her heritage, didn't know what a *quinceañera* was.

"We're leaving," Sarah said, reaching for Grace's hand. Grace let her hold it for a few seconds, then pulled away.

The girls in the taffeta gowns chatted and embraced each other.

Grace and Sarah's parents were having an animated conversation in the car. Sarah tried a locked door and knocked on the window.

"What happened?" her mother asked as the doors clicked open.

"It's just . . . not our scene."

"It was some kind of fancy party and they were playing Spanish music," Grace explained in a disgusted voice.

"Salsa!" yelled Aletha Morris. "Carl, remember when we went to that club in New York that time?"

"Yeah—that dancing—we did not know what we were doing. Those Porto Rickan cats have their own thing."

"*You* didn't know what we were doing. I was killing it that night. Gracegirl, y'all should have stayed and tore it up."

"Do you see what I'm wearing?" Grace said. "It was like the freaking Puerto Rican prom in there."

Vetta started talking fast. "Mr. and Mrs. Morris, you know you're my favorite people in the world. My very favorite people."

"I just met you," said Mr. Morris. "It strains at credibility."

"Credulity," muttered Sarah.

"My very favorite people," Vetta said.

"Spit it out, girl," said Mrs. Morris.

"Maybe we could make one *leetle* stop before dropping everybody off. My cousin is having a party not that far from you. On Vorhees near Sixty-second."

"How come we didn't just go there?" asked Grace.

" 'Cause, you know, it's not going to be anything exciting. Just a lot of *homeboys*—"

"So, a party?" Sarah interrupted.

"Yeah, and it's actually a friend of my cousin, her play cousin, which makes her—"

Mr. Morris tapped the wheel. "Who's paying for all this gas?"

"Thanks, Mr. Morris! Party in the hood!" Vetta yelled.

They cruised Sixty-second and turned onto Vorhees. All the homes, fronted by thick hedges, looked equally silent. The target house was completely dark. Feeling fatalistic, Sarah unclasped her seat belt to go check it out. Vetta pulled the hair out of her coat collar and volunteered to go with her.

A girl answered the door swiftly, as if she had been waiting on the other side. Chuck D's voice thumped up from the floorboards.

"You know Erica from around the way?" Vetta said.

Around the way? Sarah thought.

The girl shook her head.

"She said it was gonna be somethin' here tonight."

"Down in the basement," the girl said.

"Aight," Vetta said. "I'ma get my other girl."

Aight? Sarah thought.

The girl shrugged and walked away. Sarah tried to stare at Vetta in the light of the streetlamps, but her eyes were in shadows.

A shaky banister led down into the basement of 252 Vorhees, which was complete with cement floors, a dusty beam of red light coming from the ceiling, and a kid with a sloping Gumby haircut working the turntables in the corner. Even in this small, crowded space, there was a center where people danced and sides where people waited. That's where Grace patted her hair and Sarah tried to stuff her hands in her too-tight pockets. A few paces away, a nest of girls wearing bright, silky blouses and lacquered curls openly sized them up. Vetta wove through the crowd, looking for her cousin.

"I don't even see that girl," she announced upon return.

Grace, Sarah, and Vetta stood looking awkward until a tall, cute boy with a thin mustache pulled Vetta away to dance. The girls in the nest talked louder, though Sarah couldn't make out what they said.

"I wonder where the bathroom is," Grace said. She and Sarah listened sadly to "Glamorous Life," while everybody else hooted along: *"Ooh-oooh, you got it, Go! Go! Go! Go!"*

Vetta rematerialized with a partner attached to her waist from behind. Her lipstick was still too bright and her eye makeup too dark. But she looked completely different to Sarah right then.

"What y'all doin'?" she barked. "Let's go!"

The boys behind her fanned out, moving forward. The same short kid who'd been talking to Grace at Houston Hall extended his arm to her. Sarah watched him push her sister gently through the crowd as if they did this every night. A medium-height guy with muscled biceps and a sharp-looking box murmured an invitation to dance in Sarah's ear. There was one boy too many; a light-skinned boy with freckles walked away empty-handed.

Right then, as if answering a secret signal, the DJ mixed in a growling dancehall singer.

"Shit," said Sarah.

"You don't like reggae?" the tall guy asked.

"It's all right," she lied, remembering boys who had tried to bore holes into her thighs with erections while they looked off into the distance. But this one took both her hands and moved back and forth. He brushed her lightly with the bulge in his pants, then smiled, sheepish. She stepped closer.

They ignored the music that sped up, falling into a lazy sync while everybody else jerked and jumped. When the inevitable circle formed, they backed out to make sure they were on the edge.

When something caught his attention, her partner gripped Sarah's hands harder. "Go, *Shawn*! Go, *Shawn*!" he yelled. Several voices joined his. Sarah looked toward the inner circle.

Grace and her guy and Vetta and hers danced hard in the middle. The bottom layer of Grace's bangs was plastered to her shining forehead, but she didn't fluff once. She jumped higher and higher while Vetta stayed low, then turned and gave her guy her ass to dance with. A few seconds later, without breaking stride, Grace and Vetta switched partners. Grace leaped, Vetta slid, and they both went back to moving in sync with the boys. But to Sarah it seemed that they were controlling the music instead of the other way around. Something in her burst, so she clapped. When she caught her sister's eye, Grace smiled with humble sweetness.

When the lights came up two hours later, Vetta's white ruffled blouse was translucent with sweat. Short bits of her real hair prickled through the weave.

"My name is Vaughn," said Sarah's dance partner. "Can I get your number?"

Sarah's thoughts scurried about.

Vaughn was a first name?

Was his life a series of magical and exclusive basement parties?

What would they talk about?

Was he planning to go to college?

"Hey, if you don't want to . . . ," he said, and she told him he could call.

Grace was actually hugging the guy she'd been with. Then he held something out to her and pulled it back when she reached. They laughed. The second he turned on his heel, Sarah was at Grace's side. She wanted to say something to her sister about what she had seen in the center of the circle.

Instead she said, "Let's go," deciding that now her main concern was not being the last people to leave a strange house.

Sarah hung back to make sure Grace and Vetta walked up the stairs, and she looked around the basement. The DJ slid records back into their sleeves, and two girls cleaned up abandoned 40 bottles. Behind the turntable and speakers, the guys with whom Sarah, Vetta, and Grace had spent the night were retrieving guns too large to dance with.

Sarah rushed up the stairs, tripping a little. Vetta and Grace sat on a plastic-covered couch dabbing themselves with tissue. The smallish living room was bright and loud with people putting on coats and screaming farewell.

"We have to get out of here," Sarah whispered loudly.

"I called Mom and Dad," said Grace.

"Did you hear me?" said Sarah.

Just then the guys came out of the basement.

"Get down!" Sarah cried, diving to the orange shag carpet on her hands and knees. When she looked up, she saw Vetta's blushing face peering down from the side of the sofa.

"You okay down there?" she asked, as if she was trying not to laugh.

"Sarah!" said Grace, and then Sarah heard laughter, not a growing percussive wave like the characters experienced in movies about teen humiliation, but a sprinkling of titters. The bitchy girls from the basement were crowded in an armchair catty-corner to the plastic couch. They laughed the longest. Sarah brushed herself off and rose to see the guy she'd danced with. He stood in front of the couch, shaking his head.

The boys had packed their weapons into puffy down coats and moved through the crowd, saying goodbye. The short one nodded at Grace from the doorway. She nodded back, wiggling her fingers in a wave.

"Look," Grace said, turning to Vetta. She pulled a business card out of her Fendi knockoff purse. Above two telephone numbers it said:

SdJ
"Player"

It took three years to crack the code. Shawn Deviljohn: parolee, small-time dealer, aspiring pimp, sociopath, first love. He would never have been caught dead with some white people in the suburbs unless he was robbing their asses. It took three years, therapy (Grace), and prison (Shawn) to separate them.

"Throw that out, Grace. He had a huge gun."

"He had a huge gun!" Grace squealed, pitching Sarah's voice higher, whiter.

"Girl, he's not trying to shoot *us*," Vetta said, laughing. Then the laugh died, and she looked almost worried.

It was this look that did it. Though it was too early, Sarah turned abruptly and walked outside to look for her parents. She moved off to the side of the house so people could leave, but since most seemed to linger inside, Sarah stood alone, breathing steam. With an angry twinge of self-pity, she remembered Vetta saying that people like them would rule college. Now she thought that Vetta had been condescending to her or, worse, was being kind.

I don't even *want* to rule, she thought. "I just want to know what the fuck is going on," she told the front hedges in a wobbly voice. Her heart leaped when a blue Volvo resembling her parents' car appeared on the street, but it kept going. Then the front door of 252 Vorhees opened, and her sister and her friend came out into the cold and joined her to wait.

william is
telling a
story

At the beach, sunbathing women make a five-pointed star with William in the middle. Two on the left diagonal discuss his arms and eyelashes. One on the right picks up her towel and moves in closer to get a better look at his brown-gold skin. "The tide is coming in," she tells her girlfriend. William gazes over his book at the Atlantic on the northern coast of Jamaica. Peter is asleep on a lounge chair next to him, dreaming of ice-cream pops and titties.

The beach is dotted with orange-pink tourists, their stringy hair in sparse braids. One of the men even sports a couple of bright plastic beads in the bottom of his mullet. None of them seem ashamed of their dense, puffy bellies and burning bodies. There are also some black folks who William assumes are American: young like him, probably all on spring break. The people who seem to live here are hustling. Dark, skinny men pace the shoreline selling huge conch shells, while others show drunken vacationers how to jet-ski.

A small army of women carry combs and clips in homemade-looking cloth bags. They stroll the coastline, offering more damage to sun-dried tourist hair. One stoops to address a white girl lying chest down with no bikini top. William watches the Jamaican woman's bright smile and the way she caresses the girl's hair. But walking away empty-handed, she spits. She knows better than to approach the black American women on the beach.

William wonders if she would have approached his exgirlfriend, who looked sort of white but was not. She was supposed to come on this trip, but now William doesn't even know where she is. It troubles William that he doesn't really miss *her* at all. What he wants back is the way he felt when he sat with her in Ruby Tuesday, men glaring from him to her, horny and murderous. He wants back the way Peter looked at her ass when she was walking away.

William's dad would have loved this girl, would have thought she was Fine. "Taking care of business the Morehouse way," he'd have said, thinking of his own campus days. William is sorry that he missed out on bringing her home, but the person he really misses is Kelly.

Stop, William says to himself, and brings his book to eye level. It's *1984* again. William likes reading books about the future, whatever future it is. Of course, 1984 is very much over, and William was eleven then. He had a best friend named Corey, who taught him how to crack his knuckles. Corey eventually moved from Philadelphia to Atlanta to live with his aunt when his mother went to jail. On and off during the years through college, William has wondered if Corey is still in Atlanta and if he might run into him one day. He wonders if he'll have the same perplexed expression and be working on material for his appearance on Letterman. In fifth grade Eddie Murphy was new and Corey was writing down R-rated jokes about the kiss-ups at school. "They all be drunk on ass licker! Get that, William? *Ass liquor*. Don't try to bite that."

Corey, whose mom was skinny and stole, didn't always tell jokes. Sometimes he sat on the steps at recess and talked to William about the adult things going on in his fifth-grade life. There were people who called demanding to know where his mother was, and men who came by to visit her at all times of the night. While William read to fall asleep, sometimes drifting off drooling on a library book, Corey slept with a large knife under his head because he didn't know who was going to walk into the apartment.

Sometimes at recess Corey didn't want to talk at all. "I'm gonna chill. Go grab me a girl, and I'll deal with her in a minute," he might say if there was a game of catch-a-girl-freak-a-girl going. He sat still on a swing and stared into nothing while William halfheartedly ran around the yard. Those days, William wanted to sit close to him and know what to say. Now, trying to find his place on the page, William wants to believe that Corey is on spring break somewhere.

Suddenly Tanisha is close enough to sprinkle water on his face. She says, "I know y'all read that shit in the first grade at *private school*."

"First of all," William says, "I went to public school until junior high, and second, I'm not worried about how many times you read *Valley of the Dolls*, so why don't you go over there and keep working on your skin cancer?"

Tanisha laughs as though he has said something funny. She says, "Brown don't burn, baby."

William supposes Tanisha is attractive. She has small, neat

braids, full lips that aren't too big, and a decent body. She's much cuter than when they all met as freshmen working in the library. Then she had messy hair and oversize clothes. But Tanisha is easy to be with, so game that sometimes William forgets that she is a she. Not that she doesn't bore him with her occasional boy problems. Not that she doesn't complain about how not-fun it is to sit in the mall and watch the pageant of girls streaming by. But then she's the one who gets in the best jabs about the fat chicks in spangles with fake hair. Tanisha, dark and smiling, takes William's mind off things. Like the ex, who was nothing like Tanisha. For one thing, she was very light-skinned. Lighter than his mom, and even lighter than the neighbor's grown daughter whom his dad had flirted with since she was a teenager. The ex was the most solidly beautiful girl William had ever dated.

At the beach, Peter wakes up hungry and annoying. "Ackee and saltfish, ackee and saltfish, ackee and saltfish," he repeats in a robot voice. By this time William has had a Frisbee dropped in his lap and has heard an extra-loud conversation about giving head. He's turned on looking at the speakers with their heavy curls and berry lips. He thinks maybe it could work with some faceless girl here in Jamaica. But William also worries about sex with strangers. It's been almost a year. He didn't sleep with the ex-girlfriend, which is how he lost her.

"You make me feel ugly," she said once. "I don't have to feel like this, and I don't have to beg *anybody* to have sex with me."

"You'll enjoy it more if we're both ready," he had told her, knowing that she would say, "I *am* ready." He also knew that she looked more frustrated and less like she was listening every time they talked.

If only he could have always felt the way he did when he first saw her. Just at the beginning of this school year, he, Peter, and their other roommates leaned on the railing called the meat rack, watching girls. Peter saw her first. "Honey in the pink shirt," he barked. It was muggy September, and all of Morehouse was there to check out the new Spelman crop. This ritual defined college for William, along with the beautiful shock of classrooms filled exclusively with black people: some incredibly stupid and some that put his expensive education to shame. Freed from negotiating the delicate world of dating at a mostly white, if "progressive," private school, William allowed Peter and the boys to show him the pure sport aspect of getting sex. There were girls, they convinced him, who wanted to be targeted at a party, romanced with great effort, fucked for a week at the most and one night at the least. There were girls, he learned, with serious boyfriends back home or much-touted high standards, who could be brought down to earth and into your room. William went through the dance with a few women. Each time he called it quits, he was disturbed by a blank feeling. He thought he should have been gripped by something: loneliness, guilt, or the desire to do it all again. When he saw the ex-girlfriend, he decided she could make him feel what he was supposed to.

"Damn," William had said. "She's almost too much of everything good."

She wore tiny jogging shorts and a clingy V-neck, so her freckle-dusted skin was in plain view, as well as her deep cleavage. She played with strands of her reddish-brown shoulder-length hair.

William let her smile up at one of the football players, but he said "I got next" to Peter, who looked as if he wanted to say "I saw her first" or something dumb like that. But he didn't,

William knew, not only because Peter already had three or four girls in rotation, but because when it came down to it, William could always pull better-looking rank on Peter's skinny yellow ass.

Soon after, she had turned up in his psych class, and it was magic. All William had to do was sit next to her and smile, and she quickly got his number for "notes, you know, in case I'm absent." When she leaned over his desk, he saw that her eyes were almost green. They went out one night and then for four months. They didn't have sex, though.

When he was alone, he'd tried to concentrate on images of the girlfriend, her mouth slightly open, breathing hard, her naked breasts. One night he thought about asking her to take off her clothes and crawl on the floor, like something he'd seen in one of Peter's porn flicks. But he wasn't sure it would be enough. He worried that he would still think of the rough feel of Kelly's skin, the stubble almost hurting him. What then?

THEY ARE TWO MEN and two women at the Inn at Montego Bay. Earlier, at the soggy dinner buffet, Peter invited two girls sitting nearby to eat with them. Now one of them is whiling the night away in the two-room suite shared by William, Tanisha, and Peter.

The only light is a sliver under the door. The sound track is a 1970s compilation that someone put on repeat to be obnoxious. No one notices that "I Will Survive" is starting up a third time. *At first I was afraid* . . . Lying down, William raises himself every so often to pour more soda and rum into a plastic cup.

"I never . . ." says Tanisha, "cheated on a significant other."

Peter and the new woman, Lourdes, drink, giggling at each other. Tanisha nudges William. "Wake up, fucker. And the game doesn't work if you lie."

"Man, I know you better be ready to swallow the cup too," Peter says.

"She said *significant* other. I didn't say I never cheated on anybody, and I'm not lying," William answers.

"You're trash," says Tanisha.

"You're prettier in this light."

Lourdes looks nervous, but then Tanisha laughs.

Lourdes announces that she's never kissed anyone's feet.

"Hey, what kind of accent is that?" Peter asks, and William remembers his friend's quest to sleep with a woman from each census box before he dies.

"Panama by way of Vir-gin-ia," says Lourdes, adding Spanish syllables to the name of the state.

"Ooh, say that again—"

Tanisha clears her throat.

Peter offers, "I never sucked anybody's toes. Well, okay, I never licked the parts in between somebody's toes."

"Eww," Lourdes says with a grimace. But then she takes a sip.

"Aw, shit," says Tanisha. "If you're the only one, you tell the story."

Slurring and suddenly irritable, William asks, "Is there really a story there? I don't want to know what that tastes like."

Lourdes says, "How about I ask the next question? Then by tomorrow, we'll all be best friends. So here it is. I never . . . did something sexual with a person of the same sex."

William knows he doesn't have to play, doesn't have to pick up his cup or admit anything, but he is bursting out of his skin.

He can tell these girls; after all, they are girls. As for Peter, well, once William tells him, the thing will belong to the past.

"Bottoms up," William says.

Tanisha snaps, "Oh, shut up, William! You're not even funny."

"I'm not laughing." William speaks in a calm voice that he's perfected for moments like this.

Peter tries to stand, but he buckles back onto the bed. "The fuck you talking about, man?" he says in his lowest register. He glares at Lourdes, who shrugs and bites her lip.

William puts his hands up as if to push back bad air. "Do you all want to hear this or not?"

William is pretty gone at this point, so he can't remember everything about the game the next morning. But he is fairly sure that he likes the way he told it. He remembers that the more he gave, the freer he felt. Peter hadn't said anything *too* bad. "I knew it!" he'd yelled. "I told you Kelly was a faggot! I told you."

"Well, *I'm* not," said William. Then he said, "I don't have any regrets, you know. But I know that's not for me." This was what he always knew he'd say.

"I hope not, man. I sure hope not," Peter had said.

It was the first time William had told anyone. He never told the ex-girlfriend, not even the time she asked if he was gay. He had looked into her eyes for a moment and replied, "Let's say I was. What would that say about you?"

But he didn't tell them everything in that hotel room. He didn't tell them how easy it was to arrive at Kelly in his mind.

He doesn't mention that when he went to the department store in search of ties to wear at the interviews he hopes he'll get before graduation, he let a saleswoman spritz him with Kelly's cologne. That he pocketed samples smelling of Kelly.

William doesn't explain that when Peter and the other guys watch the Spice Channel, William remembers Kelly listing different flavors of pussy: yeast, cinnamon, pickles (vinegar douches), pico de gallo.

"Pico de gallo?" said William.

"Burrito pussy," Kelly had answered, and kept going.

William doesn't mention that when he hears De La Soul, he remembers that the group hails from Long Island and so does Kelly.

The suburbs, movies and TV about them, driving on the outskirts of Atlanta—all of it makes William picture Kelly's childhood home, a place he will never visit. Kelly had told him about what he'd find there—his mother with her state-of-the-art wheelchair and crooked grin; his father, who had begun planning his children's futures as lawyers and surgeons before their feet reached the floor under the kitchen table. Kelly had told him these things, but William imagines Kelly's bedroom. He has decided it is an attic with a wood smell, an LL Cool J poster on the roof slant, a large, soft blue bed, a thick-trunked tree outside with branches beckoning toward the window. It is hackneyed but true that he pictures Kelly in basketball shorts mowing the blue-green lawn, shirtless and dappled in sweat.

William doesn't have to tell them all of that, because it would only confuse the issue. He knows who he is, and he feels sure of it this morning because Tanisha has soft eyes and bumps into him no less than three times. Peter will take some tending. He predictably attempts to dress his six-foot frame in the tiny closet.

"Uh, Peter," William says quietly while Tanisha is in the shower, "you can come out of the closet."

"Ha."

"But seriously. Nobody wants your scrawny butt."

"I just didn't know what I was going to wear. It looks foggy out."

"Yeah," says William. "Foggy."

"Anyway," Peter continues, "I'm not thinking about you. I'm working out my plans for Miss Panama. And you might have to work out some things yourself. Sad to say, I think your homo story was a turn-on." He jerks his head toward the bathroom.

When Tanisha, Peter, and William emerge from their suite, Lourdes is in the lobby in high-cut shorts and a wide straw hat. She has separated from her traveling partner to hike the falls with them at Ocho Rios. Peter gives her a good-morning kiss, as if this is something he always does, takes her beach bag, and snakes his arm around her shoulders.

To William she says, "You see? We're all best friends now."

"Or potential blackmailers," he says, though he feels warmly toward the girl.

Tanisha beams. "You think that's a joke, but I wouldn't get rich if I was you."

They take up three consecutive rows on the tour bus. William is aware that Tanisha wants to sit with him, but she makes the mistake of sitting down first. He takes the seat behind her and places his knapsack next to him.

A British family boards the bus. The patriarch speaks loudly to the driver as he passes. "You can handle this mist, eh? I understand we're going to go through some rather steep hills. Precious cargo, you know," says the smiling man, pushing his skinny school-age daughter toward the back.

"A truth me a tell," the driver says without interest.

After they've been in motion for about a half hour, William sees a woman in the other row, one seat up. He notices her because she keeps glancing back at him as if she's afraid he may suddenly climb out the window. She has Marcia Brady–parted hair, platinum from root to tip. Her crossed legs barely hang on to the sandals dangling from her feet. He enjoys watching her. When he glances out the window, he is greeted by a tin-roofed green shanty on stilts, by a mural-size eroding ad for beer on a wall that doesn't separate or join anything. Women stand in front of the wall, their bright blouses and skirts clashing, William thinks, with their grim black faces. A handful of small children wave, making him feel bad for being on this air-conditioned bus. He turns away from the window, back to the platinum woman.

When he gets up to use the bathroom, William regards himself in the mirror, imagines fucking the woman in a standing position. Getting her into bed would be a coup—Peter's jaw would hit the floor. Then of course he wonders about what his dad would think. He'd always insisted that loving a "fine redbone" was what Stuart men did. ("Thanks for teaching our son to look beneath the surface," William's mom would say, but then she'd kiss them because her husband and son thought she was pretty.)

Back at William's seat, Tanisha is moving his bag onto the floor.

"Can I help you?" he asks.

"I'm bored," she whines.

"And I'm the halftime show?" He sighs.

William lets Tanisha sit by the window so he can keep Platinum in view. They talk about the future books he likes to read, and the woman shifts a lot in her seat. William, who is having a conversation with her as well as with Tanisha, is unusually eloquent. William, who always says "black," calls Octavia Butler an "African American author" and talks about the book where the main characters are rival spirits who make a sport of inhabiting different bodies.

"You are such a white dork it's not even funny," Tanisha says. She punches William lightly. "Let me use your shoulder."

Tanisha carefully rests her head against him. She pretends to sleep the rest of the way, fantasizing about a straight Morehouse man so profound that he can admit to having sex with another man. She doesn't see William look at Platinum and finally make eye contact. Smile.

THEY MAKE EACH OTHER'S ACQUAINTANCE at the Dunn's River Falls among the splashing clumps of people following guides in orange shirts to the top. The woman walks in front of William, and he gets his chance when she slips.

"I got you," William murmurs.

"God, thanks." She glances gratefully back at him and walks ahead with more confidence.

Just then Tanisha reappears at William's side, frowning. William speaks close to her ear, making her laugh. "She must think I'm one of the rent-a-dreds, but without dreds." After they climb quietly for a while, William allows himself to move ahead and catch up to the woman again. She asks his name, turning her face over her shoulder so that hair hides one of her eyes.

"Well, William," she says, as if tasting her words, "I'm Charlotte. I'm glad you're here. Else I'd be down at the bottom with broken bones."

"Nah. You'd be getting help from Mr. Feelgood up there."

Several paces ahead, a guide performs an ongoing monologue of encouragement while he reassures squealing white women with his hands. "Come ya, come ya . . . look thereso lickle babies a do it—why you scared for?"

Behind William and Charlotte a group of middle-aged black women make their painfully slow way up the rocks with no guidance except their own curses and cheers.

"Hey—don't make fun," says Charlotte. "The men here are really nice. I know my boyfriend would be at the top yelling at me to 'get the lead out' or something. Though," she says without looking at William, "the guide actually favors him a little."

"Get the lead out," says William. He doesn't outwardly acknowledge her message, finds her vulgar for sending it, but he can't deny that the specter of her black boyfriend makes him more comfortable.

When the rock path is wide enough for him to walk beside her, he glances into her face. This girl, with eyes like the green glass spots in the Atlantic, is definitely prettier than the ex. William has never hooked up with a white woman, though there were some flirtations in high school. Kelly had fucked several white girls before college, and he said you could get them to do anything. It was one of the boys' favorite topics at Peter's Thursday game night, where William and Kelly met.

The first time someone brought Kelly by the apartment, William recognized him from the gym. In both places, William noticed that he was top-heavy, like a football player. He also dressed like one. When they were introduced, Kelly wore a very red button-down shirt that set off his dark, reddish skin. William thought that a pimp might have worn this shirt.

"You go to the gym?" Kelly asked him.

William squinted as if trying to jog his memory. "Yeah. Did I see you there?"

"Maybe. My name is Kelly," he said, gripping William's hand.

They were playing dominoes, and Peter was drunk. "D.C.— Domino City style, son!" he yelled every time he scored more than five. He nearly turned the table over more than once, screaming, "Domino, *beeyatch*."

Eventually Kelly began winning, quietly scooping up bills and change.

"Where you from?" Peter asked him suspiciously.

"Strong Island," Kelly said with a wry smile.

"Strip-mall style, son," said William in a low voice.

Peter howled.

Kelly looked surprised. "Brother, we got covered malls on the Island. All the Chess King you can handle. And, um, domino, bitch."

Kelly sat next to William that night, and as it got later, more people arrived and crowded the table. Other girls from the building came down, but only Tanisha played. One girl insisted on giving William a massage.

Peter kept bothering her. "Girl, you gonna come over here and take care of this next?"

"William's really tense," the girl explained.

"Will-y-yam's really tense," Peter mocked in a high voice. "I'll show you tense, sweetheart."

"Layla, why don't you give him a neck rub? Maybe it'll loosen him up so he can suck his own dick," Tanisha said. She slammed down a surprising twenty-five points.

It was cheerful chaos as usual, the men getting louder, the women on the periphery, waiting for something. But it started to fade out when Kelly bumped William's knee with his own, didn't apologize, and then rested it there so lightly that William almost wasn't sure it was happening.

"Hey, man, we should work out sometime," Kelly said to William before he left.

As soon as the door closed, Peter raised his head from the couch where he was stretched out with Layla passed out on top of him. "Don' know aboutthat Kelly kid . . . weird," he said. Then he went to sleep.

Though they didn't plan it at first, William and Kelly were at the gym at the same hour in the late afternoons. Finally they started going in together, talking while they lifted. It took longer and longer to work out. Sometimes they left in the dark. Kelly did just about everything better and heavier. He could lift practically the entire set of plates on the leg press. William was appalled by his own weakness.

"You build up to it, brother," Kelly said.

"Yeah, yeah. Slow and steady beats my ass."

It was about a month before they decided to do the obvious and get something to eat after the workout. They sat in Pizza Hut as if it were a date, sipping out of straws. William found out why Kelly, who loved Morehouse, was only there on a semester transfer from a state school in New York. His father wouldn't let him graduate from a black college.

"I'm hoping I can make him feel like enough of a sellout jackass to let me stay," Kelly mused.

They talked about what their lives were like, about the Quaker school William had gone to in Philadelphia. There, he had been a beloved black oddity who drew for the school newspaper: vicious comics that no one seemed to understand were vicious. And they talked about the dull horror of Rockville Centre, where Kelly was the mediocre quarterback and colored mascot for the high school football team, called K-boy by his teammates.

"You got a girl?" Kelly asked finally. "I mean, aside from your groupies."

"What are you talking about?"

"Come on, man." Kelly laughed, and William struggled to suppress a smile. "You're a good-looking brother. Plus, every time I go to cards or whatever, there's all these young ladies trying to rub you down and play your hand—"

"Yeah, yeah." William waved it away. "A couple of them stay over sometimes. A man has needs. But I just haven't found . . . what I'm looking for yet."

"Sure," Kelly had said. He looked thoughtful. "So what are you looking for?"

William thought.

Kelly kept talking. "I mean, it seems like New York brothers want to keep running forever, chasing pussy and then chasing new pussy. I had this idea that men at the House would be more serious."

William felt flushed and excited by the near-philosophical level of the conversation. He said, "Man, I don't know. I've just been taking what was there for a long time, and now I'm trying to figure out who I want instead of who wants me. Now what about you? You ready to be serious?"

"Ready for some serious fucking."

William laughed in a hollow way. But Kelly looked at him hard.

William began to panic, was at the moment just before the sweat begins. He thought it would be an incredibly long wait for the check and an even longer walk home, but Kelly began abruptly laying out his Knicks predictions for the play-offs.

After Pizza Hut, William thought about avoiding Kelly, but he found that there was nothing awkward about the next time they were both in the weight room. It would have been more of a production to stay away. Kelly was always around: at game night, at parties, at a step show, where he lamented that he had never pledged. "I'm not on nobody's jock, but the Kappas are tight," he said as the Kappas stomped offstage.

William and Kelly were often alone, the only ones not passed out Thursday at 3:00 a.m., talking about their fathers: William's, who wanted his line to go to Morehouse until the end of mankind; and Kelly's, who hated all black people except himself. "He's mad backward. You would think *I* was the one that grew up during the civil rights movement."

"Yeah, well. Maybe he didn't like getting washed down the street by the fire department," William said.

"That nigga wasn't hardly in the streets. He was at business school."

They talked about their mothers too: William's, who gave him her talent for wisecracks; and Kelly's, who could barely walk after her second stroke, leaving Kelly to help raise his two younger sisters.

They talked about women. William said, "Yo, I gotta get married soon. My dad is always doing commercials for that shit."

"Woman like your mother makes all this crap worth it,"

William's dad often said after a fight with his white-collar red-neck boss. Without the woman, there was no "worth it."

"And my dad's gotta think she's the bomb, or I'll never hear the end of it," he continued, telling Kelly about his friend Helen, whom William had taken to his junior prom. He had gone with Helen because he didn't feel like dealing with the two girls who were after him that year. His mother, he was sure, wouldn't have forgiven him the shrill-voiced white girl with hair she could sit on. William's dad wouldn't have liked the other one, cinnamon-colored, with wide hips, large gold earrings, and curling acrylic nails. Later, he wasn't sure his dad wouldn't have found her preferable to poor Helen, a quiet girl who traded books and records with William. Mr. Stuart asked, "Did *she* get lucky, son?" and couldn't stop laughing. "Did you run your finger through the naps the hot comb didn't get to?"

"Oh, grow up, Anthony!" snapped William's mother. "I'm already raising William; I can't raise you too."

"No, but seriously, Wil. Tell her she's too black for those green contact lenses."

"Those are her eyes, Dad."

"She still too black."

Recalling telling this story to Kelly, William has a new thought. At least Helen was a girl.

Now it is a year after Kelly, a year of not-sex, but time hasn't passed in William's mind. For him, it is almost always junior year, the end of that spring break week. Of their crew, only Kelly and William are stuck in Atlanta, working on long papers, saving money for summer. The gym is open, empty, and Kelly is extra tough on William.

When William lies down to bench-press, he says, "It's time to put more weight on this."

They plan a blowout for the Friday night before everybody comes back. They'll start with strippers at Magic City and then brave the line at Club 112. It's Kelly's idea to get tipsy before leaving and save money on drinks. William knows a bad idea when he hears one, but he finds himself bathed in the fluorescent lights of the liquor store, a 40 under each arm.

A couple of hours later, the two of them are too drunk to go anywhere. Kelly is generous with his weed. They smoke, and then they eat Chinese food that William could barely call and order. After the coffee table is sticky with soy sauce and bits of rice, Kelly says, "Shit, I'm almost not high anymore," and starts rolling another joint.

It is too early in the season for William to have a mosquito bite on his wrist, but he scratches one anyway and rubs it against the green burlap-feel couch. Every so often the sound of spring break passes the window, women squealing, "Give me that back; put me down." From streetlights and passing headlights William can see Kelly's lips pursed, make out the gold stud in his ear, his soft, broad nose and heavy eyebrows. Kelly is telling a story about his grandmother, how she swept them all into the bathroom and flushed his boy's weed.

William watches Kelly's hands as he seals off the cigarette, sees his intent scowl. He cannot stop looking as Kelly sucks from the little cigarette. William is sucking the little cigarette. William decides to turn on the halogen lamp by the door, but then he forgets. He says, "I need to lie down." And he tries to place himself, rather than fall, onto the gritty carpet, putting his feet up on the table. Then Kelly is there on the floor, stroking William's stomach under his T-shirt. Kelly smells like cologne, sweat, and beer.

"Stop," William says sharply, but Kelly is still petting him.

Kelly says, "I just want to try something."

"What are you trying?" William asks.

William says "ouch" when Kelly touches him, even though it doesn't hurt. And Kelly says "What?" but he's unzipping William's jeans. He takes William into his mouth. William would like to be unconscious, but he is not. He imagines pushing Kelly away, but he doesn't. He quivers and shakes, and then Kelly is kissing his lips, murmuring, "It's all right, it's all right." When Kelly goes back down, William gives it all up and explodes right where he is, right into another man's mouth.

He stumbles into the bathroom, cursing, feeling like a rag used to clean up piss. On the cool floor, curled up by the toilet, William pretends not to be there when Kelly knocks on the door.

"Wil, you okay in there?" he asks.

William does not answer. It seems like hours before either of them speaks again.

Kelly says, "It's not that deep."

It occurs to William with a chill that Kelly is sober. He thinks of it because Kelly's voice is firm, adult; William imagines that Kelly sounds like his father. Then William thinks of his own family. He imagines his mother shaking her head with fierce, wet eyes, sees his father with his face in his hands.

Kelly says, "Shit, William. We didn't even do anything." Then he says something William can't hear.

Finally he says, "Look, I'm not gonna stand outside your

bathroom all night. But if you get yourself together, you know, want to have fun, let me know. Otherwise . . ."

William sits still, his heart slamming in his ears. When the front door closes, he stands and slowly pulls off his clothes. After throwing up, he turns on the shower and sits in the tub because the floor keeps threatening to move away when he's upright. He tries to think about nothing. When he's safely in bed, just before losing consciousness, the thoughts come back. He squeezes his eyes shut and thinks he could sleep for years.

BAY GARDENS is a small wooden platform behind a restaurant, where people dance close, trapped on all sides by massive potted palms.

"Reggae is not an excuse for a dry fuck," Tanisha says, getting drunk at a white plastic table. Though she hasn't danced yet, she complains about how men use dance-hall music. Scanning the club, she then launches into the locals and their pursuit of white women.

"And don't think I didn't see you today all up that girl's ass at the falls," she concludes.

"Hey—it's a nice ass. For a white one, I mean," William says.

"It just seems so wrong," she says, ignoring William. "I mean, I know the men here are just trying to play these women—you know, easy pussy *and* American citizenship. But I'm running around on the beach in a hot pink bikini, and sometimes I wonder if anybody can see me."

Frankly, Tanisha is killing his buzz. She doesn't know he's waiting for Platinum—Charlotte—to show up here and make it possible for his life to go on.

Before it gets messy, he says, "I see you, T. You look *good.* But if you stay sitting up under me, nobody is going to try anything with you. Get out there and get your dry fuck on."

She smiles and touches his head.

William excuses himself for the bathroom. He walks away from the table, listening to Buju Banton growl about battyboys. He must be joking, William thinks. There's a man leaning on the bar—and he's not unusual—wearing tight white pants and a deep orange silk shirt with several buttons open. He has thick legs, a wall of a chest, and a serious expression, but he's wearing *that?* William's not sure how you even tell a battyboy here.

On his way out of the restroom, he looks for the overmuscled man again and is not quite shocked to see Platinum with him, leaning in conspiratorially. William feels the wind whipping his bare ass under his khakis. Though he pretends not to see them, he registers that her face is soft with sympathy for whatever the man is saying.

William returns to his table in defeat, thinking that at least he can dance with Tanisha. But she is already partnered, moving at the edge of the crowd near Peter, who is practically licking Lourdes's navel in a rocking squat. When William sees that Tanisha has her arms around a man's shoulders, he suddenly notices that hers are well-shaped arms. She smiles, but not at William.

William is an only child. He's sometimes good at being alone. But not when nobody else is alone. Listening to the reggae version of an R&B song that he hates in any genre, he remembers that Kelly hated dancehall, only liked roots. He remembers lying on the floor in Kelly's room, doing nothing, Kelly telling him that only white people like Jimmy Cliff. The memory makes him lonelier.

He thinks again about earlier that day, on the rocks, when he steadied the platinum woman with his hand on her back. He imagines her in parts: jiggling breasts, wiry thighs. As far as William knows, she's still talking to Mr. Universe. With a churning stomach, William feels sentenced to a lifetime of being by himself in rooms filled with people entertaining the prospect of sex.

But then someone says, "It's the man who saved my life today." It's Charlotte, scraping the ground loudly as she pulls a chair out from the table. William jumps up from his seat to take her to the dance floor. He cannot let her sit down.

AFTER THEY HOOKED UP, Kelly mostly disappeared. He was in the gym, but he didn't hang out anymore. He spotted William and was pleasant, but it was as if only part of him was there. This was fine at first, because William was having nightmares about losing his friends and family. His mother, a social worker, was confident that her son would put other black men to shame with his commitment to nuclear family. Once, she said, "I'll never understand why our men do not take care of their children. But I thank God for your father—and William, one day a woman will thank God for you."

Then there were uncles, and William's grandfather, men who drove trucks or worked for the city, had wives, and went to church in the black part of whatever town they lived in. William remembered how once, after a Thanksgiving dinner, the family watched a black comedian mince and switch across the stage squealing "Oh, oh" and saying "ass" with a lisp. The room in which William sat with his parents, aunts, uncles, grandparents, and cousins thundered with laughter. He had laughed too.

If the Stuarts had a place for William, who fooled around with Kelly, he thought it was a place he didn't want.

"Where's your girl Kelly?" Peter had asked eventually.

"Your mom didn't mention he was a girl. She said he gave her seven inches of satisfaction." William didn't miss a beat, but he felt as though Peter could see the bruised inside of him.

The nightmares that William had at first were about how he couldn't get away from what happened. But then he became conscious of another feeling. He wanted more.

A few weeks after spring break, William saw him in the gym. Kelly, who was with a guy William didn't know, barely nodded. He didn't introduce his small friend, who lifted crushing loads while Kelly spotted him. The two of them made loud weight-room grunts. William felt himself growing angry, and also hard. He tracked Kelly's changing position in the mirrors and stalked over to him when the friend walked away to change towels.

"What the hell kind of movie are you starring in?" William muttered.

"Something for grown men," Kelly said. Then he laughed. William had nearly finished his workout, but he repeated some of his routine so he wouldn't seem chased away. The next morning, he woke with screaming muscles.

One Saturday morning just before the year ended, William was walking the campus with his dad, who came to Atlanta sometimes on sales trips. The older man loved to tell the same stories about his college days—how he quit basketball to get a 3.8; the elaborate routine of sneaking girlfriends into his dorm. He repeated the same campus lore: how the first Morehouse building covered the graves of Confederate soldiers.

"They're rolling around in their coffins now," he said. "Just dancing down there."

"Relieved to be dead, I'm sure," William said.

It was early, but the day was going to be hell hot. William's dad stopped at the water fountain near Graves Hall. William saw Kelly coming and cracked his knuckles the way Corey had taught him all those years ago. William tried to remember how it felt to sit next to Corey, if he had felt nervous or warm.

His father took a terribly long drink, and William watched as Kelly came closer. Kelly was squinting at the Georgia sun, but William could see in the slits of his eyes that they were looking at each other. Not knowing he was going to, he suddenly yelled his name.

Kelly stopped as if he'd always planned to. "Hey, man."

"Dad, this is Kelly. Kelly, this is my old man," William said, clapping his father on the back harder than he had intended.

"Who's old? Good to meet you, son."

The two men shook hands, and William remembered Kelly's death grip. And the feeling of Kelly's lips against his thighs.

"So how you been?" Kelly asked.

William wanted to knock him to the ground and kick the shit out of him. "Not bad," he said.

"You boys take a class together?" Mr. Stuart asked, and William told him about game night.

"So that's where my money goes, huh?" They made very small talk, and William felt as though he needed to breathe more.

"So, Kelly, how about joining us for breakfast?" he heard his father ask.

"No thank you, sir." Kelly smiled. "I have to pack up. I'm flying home in a couple of days. Hey, William, I'm back to school in New York. I may not see you again before I leave."

William listened in vain for something, a catch in Kelly's voice. "Oh," William said at some point.

In a quick lunge, Kelly did the thing with William where he shook his hand and pulled him into a half hug. William remembered when Kelly's knee bumped his the first time they had played dominoes. Just as it had happened that night, this day, William's father, and their plans were receding. Suddenly William was only aware of Kelly, with his black eyes and heavy lips, Kelly going away.

WILLIAM IS DANCING, and it is not a good experience. Charlotte oozes around in an effort to be erotic that makes her considerably less attractive. She shouts over the noise. "I'm not a big dancer," she says, "but this music gets to me."

Finally, tired of shaming himself in one of the blackest countries in the Western Hemisphere, he directs her back to the table. They sip tall blue rum drinks, and they don't have much to talk about. Still, they try. Charlotte is surprised to know that William is young enough to be in college. She is three years out, an assistant at a foundation in Boston.

"You know why I love the Caribbean?" she says, smoothing her skirt. "Because I don't have to wear panty hose."

"Me neither," says William.

Charlotte laughs and tells him that she is alone because her boyfriend hates Jamaicans. "He says they're all drug dealers."

William is worried about what she might say next. Then he decides that whatever it is, he won't let it ruin the night.

"I was like, what, Terrell—even the women and children? He is so narrow-minded. I mean when I first met him, I thought . . ." She seems to catch herself. "Tell you the truth, I don't think it will last long when I get back."

William looks at her when their glasses are empty. "Ready?"

She walks slightly ahead toward the freestanding portal where people enter and exit Bay Gardens. William looks around for Peter. He feels a hand on his arm.

"William?" Tanisha is there, dripping with sweat. "You leaving us?"

"Well, I'm kind of tired." The woman is getting farther ahead. He doesn't want to, but he is forced to yell, "Charlotte, hang on a second." She turns around and grins affably when she sees Tanisha.

Tanisha's face is destroyed.

William says, "Peter's still here, right?"

"Yeah. Peter would never leave me here. Especially not for some blond bitch," she hisses, and throws herself against the crowd, moving away as quickly as she can.

"What did she say?" Charlotte asks when William catches up to her.

He waves the question away.

"Well, she's a great dancer," Charlotte says. "I saw her earlier."

"You like to watch girls?" William says.

"Don't you?"

They cram into a cab, and William knows that she can feel him gripping her arm.

She only laughs that they are out of breath when they get to the elevator bank in her hotel. "We should really be in better shape," she says.

Her room smells like talcum powder. A bedstand clock says that it is just after midnight. So early to come home in Jamaica on spring break, senior year. But maybe just in time for William. They kiss as she closes the door. William plunges his tongue into her mouth, tasting rum and fruit syrup. His body is taut as he tries to freeze the moment of his desire and recall the relief he saw when he looked at her on the bus earlier that day.

She stops kissing him. "I could use a shower," she says, putting the flat of her hand on his chest.

"I like the way you smell," William says, and begins kissing her again. He moves her onto the bed.

"I take it that you're ready." She laughs, kicking off her sandals. "What the hell, I guess I'm in Ja-mai-ca." She snaps her fingers.

William insists on the lights staying lit. He pulls at his clothes as if they are sinking him and roughly helps the woman with her tank top. Their noses bump. Moving away from her face, he kisses her neck and behind her ears while she kneads his back. When he thinks he is ready, William thinks about condoms, but instead asks the woman if she's on the Pill. William always uses condoms, but tonight he needs to feel nothing blocking their contact. Then the year is over, and he is inside of her, moving slowly, then faster when he realizes it's okay. It does feel good. She makes high-pitched noises.

It does feel good, but different, because he has to concentrate on just how good it feels. Once he has this thought, it fills up his mind, and William is suddenly tired. He feels as if they've been doing this forever, but the clock says it's been only three minutes. Then he begins to move slowly. Then not at all.

"What's wrong?" Charlotte asks. "Was it the girl back at the disco?"

William doesn't say anything, just pulls away and lies on the bed, staring up at the pocked beige ceiling, the flat, square light fixture dotted with bugs. He turns his head to look at the person next to him. She's flushed in pink and white, brows raised over her clear eyes. She reaches out, and he stops her hand. He doesn't want to brag to Peter, nor to confide in his father. He has a quick, sad fantasy of comparing notes with Kelly.

"I'm sorry. I'm so sorry," he wants to say, and will say in a moment.

But just then, William cannot speak.

save me

sabbath

Welcome to Summerside Fellowship Camp.

It is a chilly July night in the woods of central Pennsylvania. You are in a cabin trying to stay warm and keep private your lopsided and tiny breasts in front of several strange girls.

"Evening prayer," barks Counselor Reba, a young woman in old-lady glasses. "Charmaine, could you lead us?"

So that's how this is going to work. As you struggle to get decent quickly (there's a prayer going on), you are further chilled by the idea that one of these nights you yourself might be forced to pray aloud in public.

". . . and in Your holy sight."

But you don't even pray to yourself! You just ask for things like grades, sunny days, the downfall of your enemies. You are only here because your best friend, the one in the bunk under you, said, "There's gonna be *boys*" and "It's just camp. We're not on our knees all day or anything."

Well, Veronica is a Christian, but knees aside, she is also a liar. You divined this earlier today when you got a copy of the week's schedule and found each day riddled with Verse Studies Christian Living Workshop Evening Fellowship.

"Veronica," you snapped, "are you sure where it says 'archery' it doesn't mean Jesus Archery?"

"Heh, heh," said Veronica, who is perfectly at home here. Not only does she attend church every Sunday, but she actually hangs out on her block with normal black kids like the ones here. And she really is a Christian.

Which you are not. Which you could not be, because you only go to your grandmother's church once a year at the most. Because your mom does believe in a Creator, but has always told you that organized religion is an oppressor's tool. When your dad says grace, which he always does, your mother might gaze up at the kitchen ceiling and say something like "I just don't know how to thank you for sticking me with the cooking night after night." She's always told you that she *does* believe in Jesus, believes that he was a person who ate, drank, and used the toilet (or whatever they had then), said some commendable things, and died.

A couple of times when your mom has been out of town for her job with the American Friends Service, your dad invited you to go with him to the church around the corner. But you felt like he was asking you to meet his girlfriend or something. So you stayed at home, finishing schoolwork or playing solitaire.

When you told your parents you wanted to come to Summerside Fellowship, even your dad looked confused.

"This ought to get interesting," he said at dinner, touching his beard.

Your mom mused that it was cheaper than the Art Museum summer program. You could tell she wanted to say more. But aside from believing that organized religion is an oppressor's tool, your mother firmly believes in applying only the gentlest of pressure in child rearing. "You have the pieces to puzzle this out," she says sometimes, holding your face in her hands.

The night before you left, she told your dad, "It's about time we made up for her heathen upbringing, right?" She grinned like a kid.

"Pass the hot sauce," he answered.

Thinking of home, you decide to use the ten minutes left before lights-out to play solitaire. You grab the deck you always carry, taking it from the windowsill next to your bed and spreading the cards over your rough, colorless blanket while Veronica makes friends with the girls below. "You know Valerie?" she exclaims. "That's my *girl!*" You've never heard of Valerie.

Reba is suddenly standing next to your bunk. "Excuse me. We don't gamble here." She holds out her hand.

"I'm just playing solitaire," you squeak.

"Sorry, hon, cards are gambling."

"Aww, Reba," says a girl named Jill who knows her from church. "You know that's not gambling."

"Yeah," says Charmaine, "I don't never hear my mom talking about no solitaire in Atlantic City."

"I'm sorry," Reba says again, sweeping up your cards with such a graceful motion it occurs to you that she handles cards a lot. Her face seems blank behind her large black frames, but her voice becomes louder. "Do these have a box?"

You hand her the box, into which she jams the cards. Then she takes two steps to the front door of the cabin and hurls them out into the night.

Christ.

monday

Last night you listened to Veronica wheeze peacefully for what seemed like several hours of your own not sleeping. At breakfast, nothing about this situation has improved. The camp director, Mr. Michael, is a heavy man with a glistening Jheri curl who sports four gold rings and expresses his gratitude to the Lord for this day of fellowship. He calls you "blessed young people walking in the Way" and warns you about the World. He lists the things you could be doing in the World.

"I won't hold back now. You could be hanging out on the streets, going to some of these parties, getting high. You could be trying out this new 'crack' cocaine, lying to your parents, getting pregnant. You could be out in the streets selling your bodies, out there selling your souls. But praise God, you're here with me. Let us pray."

With closed eyes and bowed head, you contemplate just how much more exciting life would be if you were even within striking distance of the World Mr. Michael warns about. How does one even get crack? Will pregnancy ever be a threat to you?

When you're free to pick up your chin, you look at the boys Veronica promised. Since you both grew up in a private girls' school out in the suburbs on the same scholarship, you can't remember the last time you were around so many black boys. The abundance is exciting. It's not just that your parents have made it clear that your going to the Barrett School for Girls is about a superior education and not about messing with white boys. It's also that a year of coed mixers has begun to convince you that you have the power of invisibility. The thing is, Veronica seems to have the power too, even with her large chest, shining flat hair, and wide brown eyes that don't wander the way your right one does.

The boys here are lanky or fat, one the color of a football, one nearly albino. Many have box haircuts; others clearly wear stocking caps at night to make their close-cut hair wavy. Your eyes settle on a tall boy the color of gingerbread, with plump lips and what you interpret as a thoughtful look. He is wearing a junior counselor tag, so he must be about fifteen. You look down when you feel a smile trying to crack your face.

You try to see yourself in the gingerbread boy's eyes, see your own hair in fuzzy week-old braids getting fuzzier and the colony of blackheads in your T-zone. You imagine him saying "Are you talking to me?" because he is unaccustomed to talking to someone with a lazy eye.

Activities

If you could communicate telepathically with Veronica during Verse Studies like you sometimes can at Barrett, you would ask her how to read a damn Bible. Jonah 4:8, UPC pricing codes—it's all the same. Later it seems obvious, but that's after you realize that you were in a state of panic for six days and five nights.

You practically hide your Bible under the table because it is half waterlogged, with a battered red vinyl cover. It belonged to the strangers who previously owned your house. ("Oh, that's a really nice one," said Veronica when she saw it, and the thing you sometimes love about her and sometimes hate—her huge laugh—erupted like chimes and thunder.)

You gaze at Veronica out of the corner of your eye several

times during *How to Witness to Others*, a skit written and per-
formed by two junior counselors at Christian Living Workshop,
one of the many sex-segregated activities. She looks dreamy and
distant, but not amused.

> **COUNSELOR ONE:** *All the kids at school make fun of me be-*
> *cause I don't have money to buy the latest styles. Will I fit*
> *in anywhere?*
>
> **COUNSELOR TWO:** *I have a friend I want you to meet. He*
> *doesn't care about your clothes or how much money you*
> *make. His name* (pause) *is Jesus.*

You do not believe that God could take this seriously. You
sneak glances at the other girls to see if they, like you, might be
amused. They look as if maybe they have never laughed in their
entire lives.

The wife of Mr. Michael appears. She is a curvy brown
woman, a little heavier than your mother, with a streak of silver
in her hair. Her skin, which is something you never noticed before you got a dermatologist, radiates in its magazine perfection.
Her slow smile reveals a tiny bit of lipstick on her front teeth.

"Young sisters," she begins in the calmest voice you think you
have ever heard. You know she means "sisters" the way they say
in church, but it reminds you of your mom telling a story about
"this sister on the bus" or "the new sister at work." Your body in-
clines toward her like the waxy leaves of a window plant toward
sunlight. Your body does this without your consent.

She smiles sadly. "You'll find that as you become mature
Christians, you will no longer keep company with your friends in

the World. You will find yourself saying goodbye. But you will always have your family in Christ, and in Him a greater love than any we know."

When it's time to break for lunch, you're aware of a speck of pain throbbing faintly in your stomach. Mrs. Michael stands near the doorway as you all file out. She smiles at you, and the pain becomes louder. She places a cool hand on your arm.

"Are you feeling okay, sister?" she asks.

"Yes, ma'am." You have never heard your parents say, except in imitation of others, the word *ma'am*. You have never said this word before today.

As you and Veronica head for the mess hall, you ask your best friend if she will eventually dump you because you are not a Christian.

She looks apologetic, but shrugs. "No one stays friends forever."

Friends Forever

Before this, the two of you have made it together, laughing often when it wasn't funny and doing whatever else you had to do. You got through the seventh- and eighth-grade dances by making fun of every possible thing—including how white people insist on slow-dancing to "Stairway to Heaven," when they know it's going to speed up.

You could also laugh when Mr. Morley in government explained *subsidize* by cheerfully pointing out that Barrett students on scholarship were getting a ride on the backs of the students whose parents had enough money to pay the tuition. But you laughed only after class, when Veronica said, "His fly was open," and the two of you swore to each other that you even saw the slightest shadow of a pink bulge. Ha.

You got through the fifth grade—when Molly Connell (also cheerful) kept calling Veronica "big booty Tootie"—by seeding a fairly accurate rumor about Mr. Connell's philandering. That wasn't the only unfortunate news the two of you helped circulate, but no one imagined that you were deliberate or malicious. Veronica was ohmygod *sooo* sweet, and you were *really* quiet.

Now, when Veronica's asthma flares up and she misses two days of school in a row, you feel as if you've been abandoned by your mom in a supermarket. Those days you swear you can see Margaret and KT, your nerdy backup friends, look at you with smug pity, and you would do anything to heal your best friend's lungs.

Here at Summerside Fellowship, as in real life, Veronica knows how to be. At lunch she talks to Jill about Cute Junior Counselor.

"If he ain't fine, I don't believe in God," your best friend says.

"You know that's right," Jill agrees. "The only reason we don't go together is 'cause he's my play cousin."

When you chime in that yeah, he is really cute, Jill looks too interested.

"You talk proper," she says. "You sound like somebody on TV." You want Veronica to say something, but you're not sure what. You remember the time at the Fifty-second Street McDonald's when high school boys hissed to get her attention and you were stupid enough to turn around.

"Not you—Woof! Woof!" one said.

She had tried to comfort you. "Forget them. They were ugly

anyhow." And she was right, but you knew she wanted to be happy that her carefully curled hair and red pleather jacket were appreciated.

At the night hike, Junior Counselor falls into step with Veronica, Jill, Charmaine, and you. Finally it is only him, Veronica, and you. In a whisper not covered by cracking twigs, he asks, "Do she gotta be here?" You pretend not to hear, but Veronica turns to you and says, "Meet you back at the cabin?" Her eyes plead, so you drop back several paces to walk with Jill and Charmaine.

"Have you been here before?" you ask.

Jill says, "Lotsa times. It's chill."

"Huh?" you say, because you can't hear her very well.

"Chill," says Jill. "You know, it's cool, like good." She sounds friendly, but it's insulting. Anyone who lives in the city in 1987 knows what *chill* means.

"Not the weather," clarifies Charmaine. She's the kind of girl who isn't that bright, but tries to get in a laugh or a diss on the tail end of someone else's.

You try to explain that you're not from Mars, but Charmaine is cracking up in a forced way, and you know that you're somehow supposed to laugh too. "Listen to her: *like* everybody *like* knows what 'chill' *like* means!"

You have four days and three nights.

wednesday

During a free hour in the rec room with pool, Ping-Pong, and checkers, stupid Veronica brings you melting chocolate from the camp store, as if that would make up for leaving you the night before. But now she makes plans with that guy during most of her free time, and when you try to complain, she claims that you could make other friends. For example, Jill isn't that bad.

"But Charmaine is an imbecile," you say.

Veronica rocks with laughter, scrapes her folding chair on the concrete floor, blurts out "imbecile," and laughs some more. You try to think of more funny things to say, but then Junior Counselor walks in, nods his head your way, and Veronica is gone. You scrawl your parents a postcard telling them you're going to need a new best friend.

You wonder what they're up to, your mom and dad. Picturing them at the splintery picnic table in the small, overgrown backyard, eating barbecue with Earth, Wind & Fire blaring out of the screen door, you feel a shuddering sadness. If only you could die for the rest of the week.

Bad idea. On Wednesday night, the camp sits through yet another sermon from Mr. Michael in the dim "gathering room," where animal heads sprout from the walls. Mrs. Michael sits at the piano. You have tried tuning out Mr. Michael this week, which is difficult because he is always talking. Tonight you pay attention, hoping to see whatever it is Mrs. Michael sees in her husband, to hear what she hears. What you both hear from Mr. Michael is that all but those who accept Christ as a personal Savior are going to Hell.

"I know y'all have been told a lot of things. People have told you that different religions worship the same God under different names. People have told you that Jesus is the same as Allah is the same as Buddha and all of that. But—"

The room is perfectly silent, and then Mrs. Michael begins playing a gentle accompaniment.

"*None* of that is *true*. Only the saved are getting into Heaven.

Only those of us who accept Jesus Christ as our Lord and Savior are going with us to Heaven. The rest of you, I'm sorry to say, have a date with Hell."

Suddenly he's shouting, and the piano grows more violent. Somehow his voice and the music manage not to compete.

"Don't think—*don't think* that you can get into Heaven by being a good person!"

This is what you thought.

"That's only the beginning. You can't get right with Him by just honoring your parents, by just doing well in school, not even by caring for your fellow man, by behaving *like* a Christian."

This is exactly what you thought. And the truth is, no one has ever explained it this baldly.

"That's only the beginning for the saved. Again, I'm very sorry to say that only the saved are getting into Heaven.

"So what I need to tell you is this," Mr. Michael continues. "You could die tonight."

You feel the burning in your stomach and look to Veronica. She stares straight ahead while the piano crashes. At the front of the room, Mr. Michael looks spent but confident under the serene eyes of a dead buck. You think hard about your mom, how she'd make fun of Mr. Michael's greasy shoulders. Then you lose the thread of the thought. Mrs. Michael plays more softly, an insistent, repeating line. *Leaning, leaning, leaning on His everlasting arms.* You realize that she is not singing the words, but you know them. How the hell do you know them?

You try to hear what your mother would say about Mrs. Michael. You have a feeling that your father would find her appealing. Maybe he sneaks off Sunday mornings to be with someone like her.

Thursday

Lying awake in your bunk at night, you decide to give in. You imagine the medicine-vomit taste of fluoride at the dentist's office, a stinging wasp, barking boys, and day after day at the Barrett School for Girls without Veronica. Hell will be worse than all of that. You remember the sick, lonely feeling you get in the planetarium when confronted with the starry blackness of the universe that never ends.

So concentrate on Jesus. Pull up your shoulders, clench your thighs, ball your hands into fists to get His attention. Breathe out the sound of your mother's laugh when you tell her that you are now saved.

You imagine you and your father openly attending church, leaving your mother at the kitchen table with the Sunday paper, pancakes for one, and a dour expression. You want to believe that you and your father will be able to stand against her sarcasm. It will be worth it not to go to Hell, right?

Friday

Maybe you are not saved from Hell, but a nerdy backup friend named Carl saves you from utter aloneness in the final hour. This thing started because in archery he suggested to no one in particular the idea of attaching a note about the mess hall to an arrow and sending it to the nearest poison control center. Without even thinking about it, you said you would like to be attached to that arrow. He thought that was funny.

Carl has a little head, broad shoulders, thin lips, and skinny legs. You know he likes you like *that*, and it makes your heart sink the way it might make boys' hearts sink to look at you. He does have some decent one-liners. "Is this the sound track to Hell?" he asks you as Mr. Michael's two caterwauling nieces lead the camp in song.

You wonder if Carl is saved or if you can stop passing. You could make it safer by reassuring him that you do believe in God. "It's not like I don't believe in 'the Creator' or anything like that," you could say. But you don't talk about it.

The two of you go to the camp store after dinner, where you firmly insist on buying your own ice-cream sandwich. You eat your snacks on the large porch, sitting not too far from Veronica and Junior Counselor. You hear her say that she has to run to the cabin for a jacket. On her way off the porch she swats your head, smiles big, and says, "Hey, girl!" but you know this is her way of saying, "Enjoy your date with pinhead!"

You watch her heading into the trees. Junior Counselor and his friends watch also.

Junior Counselor grunts. "I just want to tax that *ass.*"

Girls on the porch debate the merits of Philly's two black radio stations, and a group of boys console each other over Dr. J's retirement. Carl tells you his favorite episodes of *The Incredible Hulk.* Junior Counselor does not seem to see you in the semi-dark. He grits his teeth, clenches his arms as if holding something steady, and moves his pelvis back and forth quickly to a shower of guffaws.

When Veronica is in sight again, Junior Counselor greets her quietly to his boys. "Hey, big-ass." When she is close enough to hear him, he whines, "Why you take so long?"

"Well, you weren't givin' up your jacket," she says. Squealing, she allows him to pick her up, which he does with some effort.

Later, when you tell her, because you have to tell her, Veronica does what she does, which is laugh. "I'm sorry, he said—what?—'tax that ass!' He's not taxing anything!"

You are just about to tell her that this doesn't seem funny when you notice that this laugh is the one she used when she slipped at school on her way upstage during a choir assembly and showed everyone, parents and all, her too-tight version of the briefs you wear under your kilts. But Veronica doesn't take off the thin gold chain he gives her to wear—until camp ends and he asks for it back.

Finally

This is how you got through: any heathen could have answered the Bible Jeopardy questions. It's not like you've never been to church. You have a grandmother, for God's sake. You know that Jesus is the Way, the Truth, and the Life. You won for your team with "What is judgment by fire?"

After that first night, you were ready to lead Counselor Reba and everybody else in evening prayer. You were going to use the word *benevolent*, the phrase *oh merciful Lord*, and shame that woman into giving you a new deck of cards. But you never got to flow, because Reba made a general practice of ignoring you after the solitaire incident.

The first number is the chapter, the second is the verse.

On the last night, everyone gathers for a campfire. This is one of the few times when you all use the camp circle with the tall bleachers. Veronica is on your left, Junior Counselor at her side, and they seem to have nothing left to talk about. Carl is on your right, and though he's been too nervous to ask for a kiss, he is boldly moving closer. He hasn't gotten any cuter.

The fire is huge but not warming. Chilled, shaky legs hold the campers up against a vast black sky. Down in the glow of the fire is Mr. Michael, who explains that the game is to sing and pass a rock around. The song, "Nothing but the Blood of Jesus," puts a metallic taste on your tongue. When the singing stops with a periodic signal from Mrs. Michael, the person holding the rock must say how and when they accepted Jesus, and what He means to them. You can barely hear Carl for your heartbeat. He's joking about how if he gets caught with the rock, he will stick it down his pants. You are not joking with him. Your mind scrambles, but when you try to imagine what you might say, you picture instead taking off all your clothes.

Mrs. Michael begins the game. She tells how as a girl, she sat there rolling her eyes and sucking her teeth during her grandmother's prayer meetings. Once, forbidden to go to the movies with her girlfriends, trapped inside reading verses with old women, she sassed her grandma's best friend.

"He's here. Do you feel Him?" the woman had asked.

"I made some smart remark," she says. "You can imagine. Oh, I was such a smart you-know-what," she says. "But I'll never forget my grandmother's eyes. She looked like someone had kicked her."

Mrs. Michael ran into the bathroom and found herself on her knees, gasping for air. "The room got small," she says. "I knew He was with me, and what got me was I knew He'd forgive me for what I said to my grandmother. I knew He'd forgive me anything, and be with me long after my grandmother was gone."

In the firelight, you can see her drowsy smile. You can't tell for sure, but you guess that there is probably lipstick on her teeth. She startles everyone, crying out in a terrible voice, "Thank you, Jesus!"

Campers tell their stories. One saw footage of Hell in a Sunday school film and became frightened. Another was saved, luckily, just before his father died.

"He's here," says Mrs. Michael. "Can you feel Him?"

You hear all of this, though you are absorbed in desperate dreams of home, where your parents are sprucing up your room for your return. Your mother cuts flowers from the garden and makes the bed with hard new sheets. Your father helps her rearrange your bedroom furniture, as she does when the season changes. But you are not there, and the truth of the moment is this: if you don't believe what these people believe, that God is always looking out for you and rigging things so they'll go your way, then you have to expect that sometimes the worst will happen. That you may never be pretty, that Veronica will leave you, that it will be just you and your oddball parents and solitaire forever. If you don't believe what these people believe, then there is really nothing but chance standing between you and the rock, which doesn't get past your hand a third time, because when the singing halts, Carl pushes it in there so hard you almost topple.

"What's wrong?" he hisses.

You try to stop crying, and then you think, *No*. Let the sobs carry you. No one can say that you aren't being moved by the Spirit.

Veronica takes the rock and clears her throat. She tells the camp that it's not a matter of when He came, and she doesn't remember how, but He takes care of her. She passes the rock and takes you by the arm, pushes you through the stares and singing, and leads you down from the bleachers and off to the side. She offers a tissue, then her inhaler.

"It gives you a buzz," she whispers.

You take a puff, the way you've often seen her do, and smile at her in the dark. The two of you stand there shivering until it's time to go back to the cabin.

Mr. Michael announces that those who are still unsure should seek out a counselor because there is still time to come to the Lord. You also think you hear him say that counselors should tell him of those who have yet to be saved, but later that seems too creepy to be true. He repeats that no one knows the day, nor the hour. "We could all be killed this very night."

You and Veronica walk back ahead of the others. You fall asleep as soon as you hit the bunk.

AT HOME, YOU SIT AROUND waiting for high school to start. It is the same white girls' school, but who knows what could happen?

Veronica looks embarrassed when she tells about Junior Counselor's soaking kisses and his scandalous pleas to let him lick it (it's not fornication, he assured her). Practically the minute she got home, there was an irate call from his pregnant girlfriend, and that was that. You love Veronica again, though you know it's only a matter of time. For now, the two of you watch *All My Children* on her mother's huge television and occasionally go out to be with her neighborhood friends, which is okay because they're not jerks like Jill and Charmaine.

Summerside Fellowship evaporates. Less than a full week, it

seemed much longer. Your dad is amused when you talk about it. "I think you're a little shell-shocked," he says, chuckling. "Did y'all see a vision of the Virgin Mary in the pool or something?"

Trying for nonchalance, your mom asks a series of bland questions and says, "Sounds like an experience."

You do not tell your parents about when you cried.

Carl sends a letter from Reading, Pennsylvania, to ask if you will be back next summer. "Only if they drop that Jesus thing," you write. Then you crumple that letter. "Only if they stop serving possum innards," you write. Then you throw that letter away and never write back. When you feel surer of your real life, you tell your parents about the camp director's dripping Jheri curl and say he had eight rings. You do not mention his wife. Anyway, they wouldn't believe what you finally figured out—that Mrs. Michael is a powerful witch.

What is funny in company nags you when you are alone. When you cannot sleep, you try to make contact with Him. Eventually you stop doing this.

You get older and write about Summerside Fellowship Camp: a freshman comp essay about religion, a farcical sketch for extra credit in lit humanities, a glib short story in the downtime at a magazine internship. You are aware of moving closer to death.

first
summer

no one gets too comfortable at the
bus stop on Forty-eighth and Spruce. A tree or two shades the
iron bench in summer, but nothing can keep out the wet-cotton
humidity on a day like today, even this early. The gray sidewalk is
hot, the asphalt is hotter, and the playground behind the bus stop
is empty. It is eight o'clock, and Rufus is running late for work.

Rufus's job is more monotonous than anything he thought he
could do five days a week, but he looks forward to the controlled
climate. Shanna's mother's house, where he lives, has only one air
conditioner, in Shanna's mother's bedroom. When July became
unbearable, Shanna complained to her mother that the baby was
uncomfortable at night.

"I just don't think he should sweat like that," she said.

Shanna's mother said, "Well, he can sleep with me, but you
have to come too."

Then she and Shanna looked at Rufus with similar broad
faces and arched eyebrows. Shanna's expression asked whether it
was okay to leave him at night. Alba Ellsworth's face invited Rufus to walk ten paces and draw his pistol.

Rufus doesn't want to think about Mrs. Ellsworth's house,

and he wishes he had a newspaper or anything other than his hands to look at. The only other person at the stop is a girl his age reading a slender paperback. He can't read the title, but it's very long and all in lowercase letters. When the girl arrived, she sat as far away from him as she could. Rufus knows how to check her out thoroughly using only his peripheral vision.

She is long: long neck, wiry arms, and long, thin silver earrings collecting in teardrops near her shoulders. Even her breasts, possibly braless, look long under a thin white shirt. Her hair is pulled into a tiny ponytail. Rufus has known a girl or two like this. They sit at the bus stop at Forty-eighth, on the side of the fountain at the Gallery; they look as if they're waiting for someone—not Rufus—to take them away from it all. He glances to see what he can beneath the hem of this girl's short skirt, and he winds up looking at her knees, which are a blackish gray. Shanna would never leave the house with ashy knees, even though she takes care of an infant and hasn't had a good night's sleep in two months.

"You got a man. He white, though," Rufus says.

The girl does a perfect impression of someone deaf, except that even someone deaf might respond to the faint vibrations of Rufus's voice. She doesn't acknowledge him with her eyes or posture. Then the bus bears down blowing hot and heavy, and Rufus is relieved that she ignored him. He has no idea why he spoke to her. He's not like Tony and them, who used to park on corners hollering at every chicken that walked by, even ones that weren't cute. ("You ain't that cute," they'd say.) He lets her board first.

"Shit," she says. "Does anyone have any change?" She rummages through a straw basket. A stray dime rolls down the steps and under the bus before Rufus can catch it. She curses again.

"You need to step up, ma'am," says the driver, an unamused

woman with a moist face and a stiff crown of curls. The girl finally gets it together and moves toward the back. Rufus flashes his TransPass and follows. Of course there's only one empty seat, half of a two-seater. She sits on the outside of it. Rufus hates when people do that.

"Ex*cuse* me," he says.

Of course she doesn't slide over to the window, but instead turns her body toward the aisle to let him in. He is careful not to touch her as he moves by. As soon as he sits, she closes her book.

"And what if he was?" she says. She looks at him hard, but not angrily. She looks curious.

If only Rufus could be as oblivious as she was at the bus stop. "If who was what?" he says with a sinking feeling.

"And so what if I had a man and he was white?"

"Well, I guess that would be your business," Rufus says, knowing how lame he is.

"So why'd you say something about it when you don't even know me?"

"Aw, girl, I was just playin'."

"Well, it sure was fun."

During this exchange, Rufus notices that she smells sweet, like polished wood. It's different from the other riders. Summer mornings on the bus, people are armed against the heat of day, rubbed and doused in extra deodorant, perfume, and the baby powder down their shirts that leaves a telltale trace on the underside of their chins. After work, the bus smells acrid and desperate. Every day when he gets home, Rufus goes up to Shanna's mother's darkened room, where Shanna and the baby hide from the afternoon heat. He gingerly lifts the baby, sleeping or not, and smells his neck. Shanna beams in the light of the evening news.

"Yeah. I don't know why I said that. Guess I just don't feel like work today."

"It's only Tuesday," the woman says, still studying him. "Where do you work?"

Rufus sees himself wheeling the mail cart through the arteries of the huge bank where he is a friend to the black secretaries and a couple of younger white ones, invisible to the people in skyward-reaching offices, unless he messes up. Even then the message comes from the secretaries. He thinks of the cornball black guy on the seventeenth floor who has tiny dreadlocks, an assistant vice president, not much older than Rufus. The one who's all "What's up, man?" unless any white people are around.

"I work in a bank mailroom," he says, louder than he needs to. "What about you?"

"I do displays at Urbanicide, dress the mannequins in the window, make sure the sweaters look nice on tables, that sort of thing."

"That a full-time job?"

"Well, I also work the register. Kind of a waste of an art school degree."

Rufus relaxes into his seat and allows himself to brush her arm. It's not as if he couldn't work a register. He says, "I didn't know they let black folks get near the money there. They sure don't like me getting near the clothes."

Rufus has been to the store twice because somebody told him they had the hot sneakers, but he mostly saw purses for men and raggedy T-shirts that cost fifty dollars. The last time he'd been there, he found some sneakers, but they didn't have his size, and the whole time his skin crawled with the feeling that every-one on every floor—even people who didn't work there—was eyeing him. He'd crossed the doorway sensor holding his breath.

"There's only two of us there, and I'm not even sure they know the other girl is black. It's basically my job to make sure black people don't steal." She deepens her voice. " 'We think you can really help take care of our minority customers, make good eye contact, offer help.' "

Rufus chuckles at the ingenuity of that.

The girl sighs. "But you know the worst is when a black person does steal."

"Damn. That happen a lot?"

"No, but the managers make a big deal of it and start talking about 'the profile.' The real profile is these wide-eyed white girls. The store should take out a wide-eyed white girl insurance policy."

The bus rumbles over the bridge between the university and Center City. Rufus knows she will get off soon, before his stop. The bank is far downtown, just before the city meets the river.

"So you live by Forty-eighth?" she says.

"On Sansom."

"By yourself?"

Rufus thinks for a moment. "No, with my girl and her moms . . ." He trails off.

This girl doesn't seem particularly disappointed or even interested in these details. She nods and says, "You should come by the store and see what I do. My name is Delayna, by the way."

He pictured her as a Paige, Elizabeth, or even something African. *Delayna* is made up, just like everybody else's name. When he opens his mouth to tell her, she interrupts.

"Oh, I can't do this anymore," she says. "I know you, Rufus."

Rufus touches his chest to check for his badge, though he can feel it in his pocket.

She says, "Miss Collier's homeroom? Eleventh grade?"

"Shit," Rufus says, not because he knows her, but because he thought he was watching her at the bus stop. She was watching him. "Why didn't you say something? I mean, here we've been going on and on," he says, surprised at the anger in his voice.

"I wanted to see if you would remember me. I don't know why, since nobody from West ever does."

Then Rufus can see her: a broad, silent back sitting near the teacher's desk, a mushroom-shaped puff of hair. "You look different," he says like an idiot.

"I was fat," she says, stifling a pretend yawn.

"I mean, you were a little thick, but—"

"Fat," she says, then smiles down at her basket. Rufus notices a small flower of sweat on the front of her white shirt. "Anyway, it's nice to see you again, even if you do say fucked-up things to girls you don't even know. You look good."

Rufus hangs back on returning her compliment. He doesn't want to make her feel any worse about how she looked then by getting excited about how she looks now. Besides, he doesn't even know what to say. She's not fine or even cute—though Rufus knows that *somebody* thinks she's cute, and she believes it. Otherwise she wouldn't have ignored him like that, then spoken to him like that, or worn that skirt with those knees.

"It's good to see you too."

She stands. "Well, happy Tuesday." Then he hears her call behind him in a panicked voice. "Back door!"

RUFUS LINGERS in the shower, aiming to arrive at the bus stop at the same time he did the day before. It was the most interesting thing that happened yesterday, so of course he wants it to happen again. He's just interested in talking with someone new about the old days, he thinks. He stops short of admitting to himself that what he most wants to know is what Delayna thought of him back then. He'd always envisioned himself as a nobody on the fringes of his loudmouth crew. But she'd noticed.

"Rufus, you want a sandwich?"

He emerges from the shower in time to hear Shanna's mother calling up the stairs. In the fog of her disappointment at how Shanna's life is unfolding, Alba Ellsworth is both businesslike and maternal toward Rufus. He prefers to think of her as a hostess.

"No thanks, Miss Alba!" he replies through the door.

A moment later, Shanna walks in without knocking. Rufus just nods and wipes uselessly at the steam on the mirror.

"Aren't you running late?" She reties the silk scarf that covers her hair at night and parks herself on the toilet as if she's planning to stay awhile.

"I mean, Shanna," Rufus protests.

"I mean, Rufus. You spend too much time in the mirror anyway. You look beautiful."

"Handsome, girl. I'm handsome."

Back at West, Shanna had been one of the girls everyone wanted, with her small smile, soft messy hair, and hourglass figure. Her sarcastic manner hinted at leagues of give underneath. Back then, Rufus knew his place in the world and didn't try to kick it to her. Then he saw her years after graduation, looking gloomy at a crowded club where he felt drunk and confident. He monopolized her all night, soliciting the story of her cheating boyfriend, pressing closer as they danced.

Down in the kitchen, Mrs. Ellsworth packs for her job at City

Hall while Rufus leans on the sink eating cereal. She wears a gray suit with sharp edges.

"You look nice," he tells her.

"So do you." She doesn't look up from lining her lips in a compact mirror. "Is that a new shirt?"

"It's nothing special. I think Shanna got it on sale. Thank you, though." Today is the day he broke it out of the package.

Shanna's mother cocks her head. "See you later," she says, and is gone.

Rufus checks his watch and holds his empty bowl, listening to the wooden floorboards settle and the distant chatter of Shanna's morning news show. She usually dozes with the television on until the afternoon. Then she fixes lunch and watches movies on cable. On cooler days, she wheels Khari to the corner store or up to the vendors on Fifty-second Street. Usually she stays put. In the spring, when she was heavy with the baby, she was still in motion, taking classes at Community College and power-walking. Once, she met Rufus for lunch and they had a picnic of turkey sandwiches and candy bars in the horsey-smelling park near the bank.

Rufus recently made the mistake of reminding Shanna how energetic she was those few short months ago.

Her eyes flashed with hurt. "In case you didn't notice, I just had a child. Besides, you know how I get in the summer." Then she looked as if she wanted to take it back, because they'd never actually known each other in the summer.

"MAN, I WISH I had a *j* right now," says Tony, frowning down at reddish-gray sloppy joe meat, the Friday special at the employee cafeteria.

Rufus smirks. "You would never smoke at work."

Tony had played hookey so often that the class of '99 referred to skipping class as "hangin' with Tone." Now his shirts seem more aggressively ironed with each passing day. He's been employee of the month in their department so many times that Rufus has lost track.

"Yo, Tone," Rufus says. "I met this really weird chick on the bus the other day." She hasn't been at the stop since that first morning, so he needs to talk about her, even though he doesn't want Tony to know who she is.

Tony smirks back. "The day I get high at work is the day you cheat on Shanna."

"Who's talking about that?"

"You're talking about it, I think," says Tony.

"Nah, man. It was just interesting. She fixes up window displays and stacks stuff, you know, so it looks nice, at *Urbanicide.*" Rufus gives the store's name a nasty sound. "I can't even believe they let a black person work there. She's not my type, anyway. Real skinny. It was so crazy the way we met, because I was making fun of her because she had ashy legs and—"

"Rufus, nigger, what are you going on about?"

"This girl I met on the bus stop."

"This isn't a story."

"Well, you're not exactly bringing the bomb conversation today. *'Uh wush uh had a jay.'* What's that?"

"Whoa, dude," Tony says, getting up from the table. He likes to get back to work early. "I'm just trying to figure you out."

On their way out of the cafeteria, Tony and Rufus drop back to let two loud-talking suits walk ahead of them. Rufus remembers when they used to cut the token booth line or travel down the sidewalk in a straight row with their boys, nearly pushing folks into the street. Now he and Tony fall silent with something like reverence when they ride the elevator. The suits bark and gesture.

"Man, tell me when it's a story," Tony says when they get off.

They swing open the mailroom door to the sound of Eddie's oldies station. It's bad enough when Eddie emerges from the back office to sort with them, worse when he plays his music.

"What's up, boss man?" Tony says in a bright voice.

"Don't call me 'boss man,' " says lobster-colored Eddie of the thick neck. Then he smiles.

Five o'clock comes, and Rufus takes his seat on the bus. He remembers how the first-grade teachers at his school didn't give homework over the weekend. Each Friday at three, the kids poured out of school chanting, "We don't got no home*work*! We don't got no home*work*!" Now he hums the tuneless tune of it, thinking maybe he'll get Shanna and Khari out of the house this weekend.

The bus crowds quickly, but from where he sits in the very back row, he spots her as soon as she pays her fare and begins moving toward him. Just as he considers pretending not to see her, Delayna's face becomes brilliant with recognition. He can feel her smile, wide to the point of hysteria, pulling on the sides of his mouth.

He pulls himself up to flex his jittery body. "Wanna sit?"

"No, no. You worked all day just like me."

"I wasn't wearing those."

Rufus, Delayna, and a man sitting next to Rufus all look down at her shoes, high white platform sandals that showcase her skinny toes. Her legs are oiled to a shine. The man vacates his seat.

"Here you go, sis," he says in a loud voice. He's wearing head-phones.

"You look nice," Rufus tells her.

"Quit looking at my legs." She smiles nervously.

"So," he says, "want me to tell you why I said that thing to you at the bus stop?"

"Not really?"

They laugh, and Rufus means to make her laugh more, but as soon as he starts speaking, he finds himself in a minefield. He can't say she looked stuck-up, though this, for some reason, is what he imagined telling her. Instead he settles on describing the slight, uh, ashy cast, if you will, of her knees and how maybe a white person wouldn't notice that and so . . . "Funny, right?" He winds up short of breath.

She finally says, "That's deep. That's really deep. Well, you're right. White guys don't like all that greasy lotion. Or so I'm told by people who know."

Rufus feels himself curling up like a salted slug.

Delayna says, "Look, I had spent the night before at my cousin's house. And if you must know, she has eczema and her lotion smells like medicine. You are so dumb."

"Oh."

Then her eyes glint. "Don't worry. If I could be shamed by ashy knees, I would have slit my wrists years ago."

"Come on, girl. Then we wouldn't—be here."

When they look at each other, a veil falls from her eyes. He wonders if his face is as open as hers. Suddenly she squints and points at him.

" 'Well, son, I'll tell you: Life for me ain't been no crystal stair.' "

"What is that?"

"Remember Miss Barnett made us memorize that? You forget that too?"

"I had Mr. Vittorio. All we read was racing forms."

Out of the corner of his eye, Rufus sees the man with the headphones nodding at them. The headphones aren't attached to anything.

Soon the neighborhood closes in on them and it's time to say goodbye again. But Monday morning finds them together at the stop. Delayna's hair is in little straightened spikes all over her head, and Rufus doesn't know why this strange look makes him feel something like pride.

She jerks her eyebrows up and down twice. "I stayed with my cousin all weekend just so I would see you this morning."

Rufus's face grows hot. "Yeah?"

"Well, actually we went dancing last night."

After Delayna tells him about a place called Fluid, they run out of conversation. Rufus remembers burning with boredom and shame after a halting discussion of deli meat and copy orders on a blanket in the park with a very pregnant Shanna. He doesn't want to feel that with this girl, so he scans his mind furiously for something to say.

She grabs his arm. "Let's not go."

"Come again?"

"I mean, let's not go to work."

Rufus looks at her hand on his biceps until she releases him. "I have a girlfriend," he says in a quiet voice. "I told you that, right?"

"Rufus," Delayna says, staring out the window, "I'm not trying to come between you and your girlfriend. I just want to have a good day. I'm so tired of that fucking store."

"I don't know," he says, but he's already working on his line for Eddie, trying to think of a medical condition that would put you out for one day and have you back in perfect health the next. This shouldn't matter anyhow. Just last week one of the new guys took a sick day and came back with a fresh haircut and suspiciously shiny nails.

The family outing that weekend had been a disappointment. Rufus had suggested the zoo and the cool, dim Hall of Reptiles. There, Khari screamed until they took him back into the sweltering sunlight. Rufus's left shoulder ached from carrying Khari in the expensive contraption that Shanna's mother had bought them. After the zoo, Shanna insisted that they wait forty minutes to be seated at the crowded T.G.I. Friday's downtown. Almost as soon as they got their food, Khari threw up on his father. Rufus sat over a huge burger with vomit on his shirt.

"It's just baby vomit," Shanna had said.

"How I'ma sound calling in sick from the street?" Rufus asks Delayna.

They get off near the end of the line and make cell phone calls a few feet away from each other on the sidewalk. Then they eat bagels at a coffee shop on the waterfront and go to a matinee when a nearby theater opens. Rufus has never been in a movie theater this early. The horror film they watch, not touching each other, feels like a dream.

Rufus follows Delayna from place to place, ignoring the feeling that he's either reliving a date from her past or taking a test he doesn't understand. They stop in a large, dusty warehouse of a record store where Delayna drifts through the long rows looking for the first album she ever bought.

"Stetsasonic," she says. "When I was little, I used to play 'Sally' and practice the Pee-wee Herman in my room."

"Why don't you do it now?" says Rufus. He sings:

"Some people don't like the way
Delayna *walks . . ."*

Delayna pushes his shoulder. Then she says, "Now this song I *can't stand.*" The PA system plays "If You Think You're Lonely Now." She looks up at the ceiling as if she can see Bobby Womack's menacing wail drift out of the speakers.

"It was my dad's favorite," she says. "He had it on vinyl and played it even after it was all scratched up. He would make my sister or me move the needle. Wait—that's where the skip was, right there." She shudders.

Rufus says, "Song's not that bad. It's kinda mean, I guess."

"I wasn't really down with my dad." Delayna sorts through used rap CDs, biting her lip. She seems to be counting something. She stops and looks up. "Me and my sister used to call him Daddy Almighty because he liked to come down on all of us with the wrath of God and both feet too."

"He hit your moms?" Rufus asks before he can stop himself. He almost slaps his hand over his mouth. But she doesn't collapse in tears or anything.

"Not in front of us."

"You can't tell me divorce ain't better than that," he says, thinking of his own parents.

"Yeah, well, they finally did that too, but my mom has been

in the Great Depression ever since. I guess I'm not sure why people get married."

"So they can have families."

"Are you and your girlfriend going to get married before you have a baby?"

Rufus stammers, "I—we have a baby."

"Oho." Delayna looks shocked. "You don't just have a girlfriend. You have—"

"Don't say it," he says.

A couple of weeks after Khari was born, Rufus had come home late from work. He'd told Shanna that he was going to drop by his mother's, but the message hadn't made it to Mrs. Ellsworth, who sat in the kitchen sipping a can of beer, her eyes dark tunnels.

"My daughter may not be your wife, but she is the mother of your son," she said. "She is not your *baby mama*." He had been calling Shanna that since he found out she was pregnant and had never thought twice about it.

Delayna says it now, even though he warned her not to.

"Fuck that," he says. "Would you want somebody calling you that?"

When she asks if the baby is a boy or a girl, Rufus recites Khari's sex, name, age, and birth weight, and then he runs out of things to say on that subject.

Delayna shows him one of the store's few 45s. "You know this one?" she asks.

" 'Me and Mrs. Jones'? Please. My father didn't take WDAS when he left."

"You know what it's about?"

Rufus is annoyed by this line of flirtation. It's like a movie where every little thing is a sign of something else happening. Grape juice spilling on the table while people argue.

"Dude hooks up with a married woman," he says.

"No, it's about drugs. A *jones*."

Rufus thinks sometimes people are too smart for their own good.

It's almost five o'clock—after lunch, ice cream, and Rufus's first visit to the Afro-American Museum—when he makes his second lying-ass call of the day, this one to Shanna. He tries to think of what men say when they're going to be late.

"I'ma grab a beer with Tone and them."

"Tony doesn't drink. So you're gonna come home high," she says, sounding exhausted. Rufus wonders how tiring it can be to lie around all day.

"No—well, what if I did come home a little buzzed?"

"What if I decided to get a little buzzed and breast-feed your son?"

Blood rushes to Rufus's ears. Not many men would do what he's done for Shanna. Tony let his baby's mother move to Cleveland after they'd been going together on and off for two years. Shanna would never leave, but if Rufus got his own place and sent the occasional check, she and her mother would be too proud to do anything about it.

"Well, maybe if you got him high, he might *do something* instead of lying around shitting himself all day long."

"What?" Shanna says. "You sound crazy. Do what the fuck you want." She hangs up. Because Shanna herself hates few things more than being hung up on, this is her way of winning a fight. If Rufus lets her do this and acts chastened later, the fight is over.

"That didn't go too well," he tells Delayna.

"What'd you tell her about me?" she says.

Rufus looks at her.

"Well, we're not doing anything."

"So there's nothing to tell."

They catch a bus Rufus has never ridden to the apartment near the Art Museum that Delayna shares with two college friends. None of them do art for a living. A drawing tacked to the wall over the couch depicts Rittenhouse Square Park in full bloom. Even in just black pencil, it looks as if Rufus could climb into it.

"You do that?" he asks.

"No." She looks as if she's trying not to smile.

"That shit is fly. Don't be shy, girl."

"No, I really didn't do it. Hey, you want that beer you said you were gonna have?"

She pulls longneck bottles and limes out of the kitchenette refrigerator and brings them to the counter. Rufus sits on a hard stool on the other side.

"So," she says, stuffing a chunk of lime into her beer, "I'm going to answer your question. Your accusation. I don't have a man. But there is a guy, and he did that sketch."

"White guy?"

"Do you actually care about that stuff?" She looks at him as if she's a bad kid.

He cares that there's a guy. "No, not really. So what's the deal?"

"The deal is, I know he likes me, but it might just be in a friendly way. I can't tell if he would date a black girl or not."

Rufus asks the appropriate questions, and Delayna talks for

nearly an hour. She tells him about the time their hands brushed, and the private joke they have about the managers. She says that he gets just as mad as she does about how the store treats black people, and that he really knows his hip-hop. Just like every teenager in Japan and redneck in Indiana, Rufus thinks.

"Is he single?" Rufus asks, now wondering what godforsaken slow-running bus he'll have to take home. It is to preserve his pride that he drinks slowly instead of fleeing the apartment to wallow in confused embarrassment.

"Well, he never talks about a girlfriend or anything."

Delayna takes a break. They move over to the couch to watch a rerun of a sitcom she likes. Rufus clears his throat when it ends.

She says, "You can't go yet. I'm not done telling you my stupid problems. You know, I didn't get to do all this in high school, when you were dating cheerleaders and going to basement parties every night."

"You wearin' me out, girl." Rufus doesn't tell her that the only cheerleader he ever dated was Shanna, long after she'd outgrown her miniskirt and thrown out her pom-poms.

"So in order to find out what he's about, I guess I gotta make the first move."

"There you go."

"But I'm scared."

"Scared, what? Maybe one day, while y'all are following the same poor black person around the store, you could bump into dude and whisper, 'Jimmy Bob, can I holler at you for a minute?' "

"His name is Zack. And you're stupid."

"What about: 'Hey, duuuuuude, going to the Boobystank show?' "

"Could you please help me?"

"Help you do what? You a modern woman."

"Listen, let me put it this way: I wouldn't know what to do with it if I got it."

"If you got a white boy?"

"Are you gonna finish that?" She points at the half-full bottle that Rufus holds on his lap, since there is no coffee table. He puts the bottle on the floor, folds his arms, and looks at her.

"I'm a virgin, okay?" she says, lowering her voice as if her neighbors are at the walls, ears pressed against drinking glasses.

Rufus makes a face at the stupid joke. "Delayna, come on."

"Seriously."

He laughs. "But you went to art school—I'm thinking they have orgies and shit. But before that even. That's bananas!"

"Thanks."

Delayna plays with the TV remote, flipping past the evening news show that Shanna watches.

He takes a risk. "I mean, the two heaviest girls on my block had babies by the time they was twenty."

She looks at a spot above his head, and her somber expression squeezes his heart.

He touches her shoulder. "I'm sorry I called you bananas," he says. Rufus began lying about sex at fourteen. He didn't actually get in there until two years later, and he still remembers his relief when it was over and he could tell his boys about it.

"Whatever," she says, but her shoulder relaxes under his palm.

Rufus has never understood the fuss about virgins. In his experience, they just said "ouch" more than usual and didn't know what they were doing. But with this girl, because of the history they share, he begins to get it. He pictures her round shoulders straining a red sweater at West. He can see himself in the back of the classroom with Tony, laughing louder than anything could be funny. Now he and Delayna have melted into their true selves. Even though she continues to chatter about that fool at her job, and even though she might not know it, she has been waiting for him all these years.

"This was a good day," he tells her.

"Thanks for listening."

"Ain't no thing."

Rufus leaves with her number and fireworks going off inside of him. He readjusts to wry and irritable when he walks into Shanna's mother's house, where Mrs. Ellsworth writes checks at the dining-room table and Shanna feeds Khari. The baby looks up.

"Don't get distracted," Shanna says, nudging him back to her breast. "Hey, Rufus."

"Crackers," Rufus says. "Keeping me late."

"I thought you were going out with Tony."

"I was gonna." Rufus is surprised that he doesn't pause.

Mrs. Ellsworth peers over her reading glasses. "Good thing they give y'all overtime."

"Not enough," he says, then decides to talk less. He walks into the kitchen and peeks into a microwave dish of rice and soggy green beans.

"I don't think there's any fish left," calls Shanna. "I thought you might get something with Tone and them."

For the next few nights, Rufus enjoys sleeping alone. At first he'd missed the pressure of Shanna's breasts against his back and even her prim snoring. Now he sees the swing of Delayna's earrings as she turns her head, and he imagines his hands on her bare thighs. He likes to remember how she touched his arm and asked him to spend the day with her. He becomes hard thinking about how she wanted it enough to talk past his objections. But each time he thinks of dialing her number, he has a vision of the digits in an entry on his cell phone bill, which is in Shanna's name. After several days of not calling or seeing the girl, Rufus begins to feel foolish and alone again in his bed.

When Tony asks, "Whatever happened to that girl on the bus?" it has been nearly two weeks since Rufus went to her apartment.

Wishing Tony wasn't looking at him so intently, Rufus says, "Humph. You know who she turned out to be?"

"A man?"

"You remember that big girl used to sit at the front of Miss Collier's homeroom?"

"Which one?"

"Delayna Thomas."

Tony twists his face in concentration. "You say she was fat?"

"Used to be."

"Nah, can't place her. So is that why you didn't hit it? Because you found out she used to be heavy?"

"I don't care about that," says Rufus. "But I do care about my girl and my son." Since Tony doesn't flinch, Rufus admits that he hasn't seen the girl in two weeks.

"She'll show up," Tony says with a grave look. "Rufus, man, all it takes is one false move."

"The fuck are you so wise about now?"

"Okay, nigger," says Tony, and the two barely speak for the rest of the day.

When Rufus gets home, Shanna is lying down in her mother's room, mouthing along with a puppet video that she swears is Khari's favorite. She looks embarrassed when she sees Rufus in the doorway. The baby sleeps in his crib. Rufus walks over to the bed, sits down, and begins kissing her.

"Hello?" Shanna says between kisses.

Rufus cradles her face and kisses her more insistently. She puts her arms around his neck and kisses him back with a probing tongue. Then she pulls away. "Not in my mom's bed," she whispers.

They have quick sex in Shanna's room, where she won't let Rufus turn on both fans, because then they can't hear the baby. The air is heavy in a way that seems sexy right until the moment Rufus comes and starts to fade into a disappointed sleep. Just before he goes under, he can hear Shanna speak his name, as if from a great distance.

He sleeps for nearly three hours and jerks awake in darkness, feeling sick at the thought of the house buzzing productively around his sleeping body. When he goes down the back stairs into the kitchen, he bumps into Mrs. Ellsworth, who is still in her work clothes, washing up the breakfast dishes.

"Rufus." She nods.

"How you doin', Miss Alba?"

"Oh, a little behind schedule tonight, but that's okay."

"Want me to run out for sandwiches?" Rufus says, realizing that he's starved.

"I have to cook this chicken tonight," she says.

"Can I help?" He has asked before, but now he means it. He doesn't feel like sitting with Shanna.

"You know how to clean a chicken?" Mrs. Ellsworth asks.

"Sorry," says Rufus. Through the doorway he can see into the living room, where Shanna is reading a magazine and Khari gurgles at the plastic planets at the top of his swing.

"But you can learn," says Mrs. Ellsworth. "Right?"

"Right," says Rufus.

She outfits him with an apron that says LOVE ME LOVE MY FOOD and tells him how she learned to fry chicken from her grandmother. This is why her chicken is so spicy, she explains. Her grandmother killed her taste buds spitting snuff, and she could only taste peppery things.

Rufus plunges his hands into the plastic bowl filled with water and cold chicken. It feels good to preserve part of him away from the moist heat of the kitchen. Shanna's mother shakes flour, chili powder, paprika, and breadcrumbs in a plastic bag. "Next time you can measure out the batter," she says.

"But you didn't give me measurements," he says, but she only laughs.

"Hey, Rufus," she begins, and he knows that she has chosen this moment. "You know, I wouldn't mind watching the baby on Saturday night if you and Shanna want to go out somewhere. Y'all haven't been to the movies or anything in a while." She licks her lips quickly and faces him with eager eyes.

"You don't have to do that," Rufus says.

"Young people need to go out. Shoot, old people need to go out," she adds. Rufus knows that Mrs. Ellsworth likes her occasional Saturday night.

"I appreciate it."

"Don't forget to wash that raw chicken off your hands before you touch anything in my house," she says.

That evening, they clear the dining-room table of bills and eat as a family. Rufus and Shanna congratulate Mrs. Ellsworth on her chicken, not yet knowing that spices will travel from Shanna's milk to Khari's stomach and keep him up. Later, when the baby's screams fill the house, Rufus is already wide-awake, staring into the darkness and regretting the nap he took earlier. He dreads the morning.

Delayna is at the bus stop when the next Friday comes. This sick day is his idea.

DOWN ON THE HARD futon, kissing her sweaty face, Rufus wonders if the white boy is a ruse. "I won't feel so weird if I have some experience," she'd said. "You won't really be cheating," she'd said. "More like a public service." "I'm just kidding," she'd said. Now she holds on, pushing her mouth onto his again and again. She's not a virgin at kissing. She stops.

"This isn't right," she says.

An oscillating fan blows past them twice in the silence. We don't got no homework, he thinks, but he doesn't say anything. Talking could ruin everything.

Some revelation takes hold of her, and she falls heavily back onto him. This could take all day, Rufus thinks. It just about does. But for the first time in ages, he is exactly where he wants to be. He pushes his nose into her neck, the sweet wood smell flooding him.

She says "ouch" a lot, and they waste two condoms she got from her roommate's bedside drawer. After, they take a lukewarm shower, dry off with the same towel, and lie down, the sun growing redder and the fan blessing them each time it blows their way.

Rufus has had better sex. He remembers the first few times

with Shanna. He's almost sure he knows when he gave her Khari, because he felt as if he'd been through something sweet and harrowing. Still, as he runs his fingertips up and down this girl's arm and listens to her loud, jagged snore, he doesn't want to leave. Before he pulls himself up, he leans in to rub his nose against her cheek. Her eyes flutter open briefly.

"Now you know a little something," he tells her.

"It was a nice public service. I'll talk to you later."

"I have more sick days," he says to the sleeping girl.

THEY DON'T HAVE ANYTHING, so they never agreed on a protocol in case they ran into each other. But Rufus knows if he ignores Delayna, she'll follow his lead, and Shanna will miss the whole thing, even if she recognizes Delayna from West. Rufus isn't one of those guys who want to get caught. It's true that he suggested Fluid, but Delayna had been there almost a month ago, on a Sunday. Totally different party.

Even as he sees Delayna there at the bar, a strip of her back bare between a halter top and another one of her endless array of short skirts, Rufus knows that this is not like the time he was with Tony and Tony's baby's mother at the movies when they ran into some girl Tony had on the side.

"Oh no you didn't," the girl said to Tony with the excited look of someone who enjoyed scenes like this. "Anthony, you don't *even* have enough to go around."

Laughing because they had to, her girls pulled her out of the lobby. Tony's girlfriend looked as if she wanted to die. She moved to Cleveland a month later.

Rufus relies on his peripheral vision to track Delayna's movements, until Shanna turns around so he can grind on her from the back. Then he can move his head, and he sees Delayna talking to a diminutive white guy with dreadlocks. It doesn't make Rufus feel better that Zack is short. He pulls Shanna closer.

Delayna and the short boy move out to the dance floor with a crew of people, just the type he imagined: a busty white girl with smudged eye makeup, a very light-skinned black girl, and a guy who looks Indian. Delayna meets Rufus's glance for the quickest flicker, but her eyes don't say a thing. The light-skinned girl starts moving against her as if they were strippers.

Shanna watches Rufus watch. "It's a damn shame nobody told those girls they were black," she says.

Rufus shakes his head in solidarity. When Shanna leaves to use the bathroom, he heads toward the bar, keeping his eye on the dance floor. Now the two other girls dance with Zack while Delayna slinks around the other guy. He's from Trinidad, Rufus remembers. He's the one at the job she knew *would* date a black girl. They keep doing the same thing. He goes down, down, down. Then comes up. She goes down.

Shanna reappears at his side. "Wasn't this nice of my mom?"

"Sure was. I was starting to feel like we were her age."

"I do miss my baby, though."

"You won't miss him this time next Saturday night."

"Rufus, don't you like him better now?"

Rufus wants to act as if this is a crazy question, but he looks directly at Shanna. "I love him." He kisses her forehead.

She slips her hand into his pocket. "Let's dance some more."

At one-thirty, Delayna and her friends are in the center of the floor, and she clings to the Trini guy. Rufus tells himself that she's drunk, but he hasn't seen her with a drink. He tells himself that she's trying to make him jealous, but he knows, he knows, that's not the case. She is celebrating, and this makes him sweaty with rage. More than once, he risks making eye contact with her. When he succeeds, she makes a slight frown and shrugs. Then she faces her dance partner with a wild smile. Rufus knows the smile.

"I'm all danced out," he announces, grabbing Shanna's hand and pushing her toward the exit. He can't resist one look back at the dance floor, where Delayna sucks face with that man as her friends circle them, hooting.

Shanna pulls her hand out of his. "Ouch, baby. Nobody's gonna snatch me."

When they get home, Rufus moves deliberately. He pours two glasses of water, but runs the tap to chill it first. He follows slowly behind Shanna, who runs up the stairs, excited to see Khari. He even shuts the door to his room slowly, but he is in a hurry.

Rufus puts both fans on high, pulls a damp piece of paper out of his wallet, and dials her number. "What did I do to you?" he asks the machine, his voice shaking. "*What did I do to you?*"

"Rufus," says Shanna, "who's on the phone?" The fans hid the sound of her approach. She stands in the doorway wearing tight pants and a tube top, the baby at her hip making sucking noises. Her eyes are glazed with terror.

Rufus hangs up. Though he's sure it's close to ninety degrees in the room, he shivers. But he can guide them back from the precipice. He knows it doesn't matter what he says, as long as he doesn't tell the truth.

"It's Tony. Well, it's his machine," he says. "That nigger owes me money."

Shanna's face breaks into a smile of relieved sadness. "You actually loaned Tone money? Rufus, how are we ever gonna get our own place?"

"We will. We'll put Khari in commercials."

Shanna's smile eases into something happier. She holds the baby up in front of her, his fat legs dangling. "Are you pretty enough to be on TV? Yes, you are. Are you as pretty as your daddy? Yes, you are."

"I'm handsome," Rufus says.

"I came to tell you I had a good time tonight. I think we're going to sleep in here if you don't mind," Shanna says.

This is a story, so it could end in any number of ways. I could say that in this moment, Rufus saw in Shanna the family he had chosen, and saw what was good in their two faces in Khari. That Khari would one day become Rufus's best thing and hold them all together like mortar. And I could say that a feeling welled up inside of Rufus that was more sweet than bitter, and in fact that the bitter only made it sweeter. And that he, like so many before him, traded a selfish passion for loyalty, monogamy, and family. Or I could say that Rufus and Shanna separated like adults and raised their son so he knew that they adored him and respected each other.

But the truth is, they all staggered on together, in spite of that meeting at the bus stop and those fevered weeks ending in a despair that made Rufus's body hurt, in spite of the fact that that thin, dreamy girl was only the first.

acknowledgments

Special thanks to Elizabeth Dalton, my first writing teacher. Many thanks also to Elizabeth McCracken, Andrew Friedman, Ellen Levine, Lorin Stein, Kevin Doughten, and the Southern Inn Summer '05 Writing Group. You made it happen.